BLACK HAT, WHITE WITCH

BLACK HAT BUREAU

HAILEY EDWARDS

Edited by Sasha Knight
Copy Edited by Kimberly Cannon
Proofread by Lillie's Literary Services
Cover by Damonza
Illustration by NextJenCo

BLACK HAT, WHITE WITCH

Black Hat Bureau, Book 1

Remember that old line about how the only way out of "the organization" is in a pine box?

Well, Rue Hollis spent ten years thinking she had escaped the Black Hat Bureau, no coffin required.

Then her former partner had to go and shatter the illusion by showing up on her doorstep with grim tidings. As much as Rue wants to kick him to the curb, she agrees to hear him out for old times' sake, and what he says chills her to the bone.

The Silver Stag was the most notorious paranormal serial killer in modern history, and Rue brought him down. Now a copycat has picked up where the Stag left off, and the Bureau wants her on the case. She beat the Stag once. They think she can do it again. But they don't know she's given up black magic, and she's not about to tell them. White witches are prey, and Rue is the hunter, not the hunted. Always.

But can she take down the protégé of the man who almost beat her at her black witch best?

If she wants to keep her new town, her new home, her new *life*, then she has no choice but to find out.

1

As I backed into the shop with a smoothie balanced on my latest bookish obsession, a romance between an owl shifter and a mouse shifter, I was greeted with screams and curses. Not literal curses. These days, I surrounded myself with human women who would clutch their pearls to learn I considered them a part of my makeshift coven. The uncomplicated circle of friendship satisfied the gnawing ache for community bred into all witches, allowing my power to slumber where it couldn't hurt anyone.

Where *I* couldn't hurt anyone.

Else.

"Rue." Arden gripped my shoulders then marched me to the counter. "You *ruined* my cobwebs."

"I heard what you did there." I coughed up a wad of her artificial cotton decor. "What is all this?"

Stretchy cobwebs. Rubber spiders. Ceramic skulls. Foam tombstones.

"Halloween." Camber escorted a life-size plastic skeleton to the door. "It's a few days away."

"I forgot." As if any witch worth her salt didn't shiver at the thinning of the veil between worlds on that night. "I also forgot approving this expense."

They were both in college, happily living off ramen, with no extra pennies to rub together.

The tab for this decorating spree was definitely ending up on my desk. Probably with a *thud*.

Holiday spirit wasn't topping my to-do list. Heck, it wasn't even on my to-do list.

With the shop approaching its five-month anniversary, I was more concerned with keeping the lights on.

"All the other shops on Main Street are decked out for the ghost walk. We need to look spooky to lure in new customers." Arden returned to futzing with her cobwebs, careful to lock the door first this time. She could unlock it *after* the way was clear to avoid strangling any potential customers. "We need refreshments too. Mayor Tate expects us to man a table on the sidewalk."

Mayor Tate and her expectations could kiss my full moon, considering the cost of rent downtown.

And yet...

The better I fit in, the longer I could stay, and I didn't just mean in this prime location.

"I have that wonky folding table left over from the grand opening." I bought it for twelve bucks at a thrift store. "Email me your Pinterest links—" we all knew they had compiled a list for this ambush, "—and I'll pick up the ingredients." I also scored a two-dollar glass punchbowl with matching ladle on the same bargain hunting trip. "I'll make lime sherbet punch too. Or should that be *slime* sherbet punch?"

The girls routinely flooded my DMs with recipe requests for the long nights when I did my best to stress bake away my insomnia. Mostly food trending on social media. The number of snacks I sent home with them explained why they were cool with living off ramen. Because, really, they weren't. They were living off *me*.

And I didn't mind one bit. I might be cheap, but I was doing okay. I could afford to indulge them.

The urge to mentor, provide, and assist the young was carved into my bones. These girls fulfilled a need in me, one usually satisfied by training novice witches, and I had to keep investing in these girls, in this community, to scratch that itch.

"That's the spirit." Camber patted me on the head. "And, yes, the pun was intended."

"Downtown has its traditions," Arden agreed. "We need to cater to them to hold our spot."

Our spot because these girls had worked for me the last four years, ever since I arrived in Samford, Alabama.

The old location of Hollis Apothecary was in my kitchen. This was a definite step up from selling online, though we still offered shipping through the website. Whether I could afford brick and mortar long term was a different kettle of fish, but I had saved up enough for a year at our current swanky location.

Our dream had seven months until its expiration date unless a miracle occurred between now and then.

"Oh." Arden gusted a dreamy sigh. "Hell-o."

"I didn't pay extra for a glass storefront so you could stalk hot guys as they walk past." I polished off my breakfast smoothie then tossed it in the trash. The romance, I took to my office for later. When I returned, Arden hadn't budged. "Have you no shame?"

"Let me check." She patted her pockets. "Nope." Then pressed her nose to the glass. "I'm fresh out."

"I wanna see." Camber set down a bucket of spiders and joined Arden at the window. "Holy Mother."

Their breath fogged the glass, obscuring my view of this perfect specimen of manhood.

Given their ages, he was probably late teens or early twenties. I owned older T-shirts. That I bought new.

"Crap on a cracker." Arden stumbled back, bumping into Camber. "He's coming this way."

"The way you two were gawking at him," I said with a snort, "I can't imagine why."

Poor guy probably thought they were trying to get his attention, maybe to hand out free samples.

"Everyone." Arden smoothed the white blouse that topped her smart black trousers. "Act natural."

Chuckling as they jostled for the prime spot nearest the door, I sat on the floor behind the counter.

"I'm going to inventory the dried flowers," I announced as I got comfy. "Practice safe sales, ladies."

Neither laughed at my joke, but I doubt they heard me over their racing hearts.

The frantic *ba-bump, ba-bump* set my fingers twitching, but I made fists until I got it under control.

Usually, I blocked it out, but the louder their hearts beat, the harder my stomach clenched with hunger.

I'm a white witch. I'm a white witch. I'm a white witch.

A metallic rattle brought my head up, but I couldn't see the entryway over the counter.

"What in the...?" Arden groaned as if the world was ending. "I forgot to unlock the door."

Metal clicked, and the door jiggled, but the lock was bad about jamming.

Getting that fixed really was topping my to-do list.

"Get out of the way." Camber's low heels clicked on the linoleum. "Let me do it."

Winter rosebuds.

Inventory.

Focus on that.

Not their rising panic Mr. Perfect would give up on them and leave before one or both got his number.

Winter rosebuds.

They kept disappearing from under the register. I trusted Arden and Camber, but I would have to check the security feed, see if I could figure out who, or what, was helping themselves to those specific items.

Glass rattled when the knob smacked the pane beside it, and I crossed my fingers neither one cracked.

"Hello," the girls chorused. "Welcome to Hollis Apothecary."

"The sign says you're open," a silky voice spilled into the store. "I'm not interrupting your break, am I?"

A hard thud shook my ribs, and all of a sudden, the only heart I heard was my own.

Ba-bum, ba-bum, ba-bum.

Murmuring a soft spell under my breath, I forced my pulse to slow and match Camber's less frantic beat.

"Interrupt me anytime." Arden hiccupped with nerves. "I'm Arden."

"I'm Camber," her best friend cut in. "You didn't interrupt our break."

"I was decorating—" Arden hiccupped again, "—for Halloween, you know? I was working in the entryway and forgot to unlock the door after I finished. I'm *so* sorry for any inconvenience."

A midnight chuckle caressed my ears as he humored the girls. "Does Rue Hollis work here?"

"She's our boss." Camber took over the awkward exchange. "Let me get her for you."

"We have a new line of hand lotions." *Hiccup, hiccup, hiccup.* "Would you like a sample?"

Poor Arden fumbled her sales pitch while Camber, who could usually be counted on to rescue her from a bout of anxiety, rounded the counter and cut her eyes at me.

"Who is he," I mouthed. *"Get his name."*

"I forgot to ask," she called out, all smiles. "Who should I tell her is here?"

"Asa." His footsteps thumped closer, until I smelled the sweet-burning smoke of rich tobacco and almost tasted the bite of ripe green apples. "Montenegro."

The blood drained from my face in a dizzying rush, and I shook my head once.

"Be right back." She strode into the office, waited to the count of ten, then returned. "She took an early lunch." She held up a note I wrote earlier in the week. "I'm so sorry, sir. I didn't hear her leave. She must have gone out the back."

"Can you give her my card and have her call me at her earliest convenience?"

"Of course." She resumed her post beside me. "I'll pass it on as soon as she gets back."

"I'll be in town for twenty-four hours," he murmured. "Can you tell her that too?"

"Sure." Camber dialed up her sincerity five degrees. "I'll do that."

His footsteps receded, and I took my first easy breath since I heard his voice.

"Rue," he whispered for my ears alone. "You can't run forever."

The door opened, triggering a chorus of ghostly moans Arden must have rigged, then shut behind him.

Only after Camber gave me the all clear did I draw my legs into my chest and rest my face on my knees.

Slender arms encircled me as Arden knelt beside me. "Who was that guy?"

"The boyfriend?" Camber sat across from us and rested her hand on my thigh. "He found you?"

Of all the lies I told when I moved here, I regretted spreading the story about running from an abusive ex the most. The cover had done its job, rallied my neighbors behind me. They looked out for me, giving me extra eyes on strange vehicles spotted on our dirt road, lurking near my house, or passing through town.

Their aid allowed me to stay in one place, to put down the shallowest of roots, but it wasn't freely given.

I had stolen it, and I couldn't give it back.

The store had been a mistake. I saw that now. I thought I was safe. Clearly, I was wrong.

"He left you this." Camber passed me the card. "It's blank."

Black ink spilled across its face in curling handwriting for my eyes only.

Special Agent Asa Montenegro

Black Hat Bureau

"You're shivering." Arden put her arm around my shoulders. "This is our fault, isn't it?"

"We pushed you into a physical location." Camber lowered her head. "That's how he found you."

"We don't know that." I used the counter to pull myself to my feet. "Girls, this isn't your doing."

I ought to have known better, I *did* know better, but I also wanted to pretend this was my real life.

"What will you do?" Camber stared out the glass storefront. "What should *we* do?"

"I'm going to pretend this didn't happen." I shredded the card into tiny pieces to void its tracking spell. A fire would have worked best, but the agent already knew this location. The trash was safe enough. "That goes for you too." Black Hats were forbidden to harm humans. "He said he's in town for the day, right?"

"Yeah." Arden shuffled in place. "You should go home once the coast is clear. Maybe stay there a few days."

"I wouldn't want that creep to catch you out in town," Camber agreed, "or to follow you home."

Closing my eyes, I pictured my go bag, the one I kept in the closet by the front door. I had money in the front pocket, three changes of clothes, a pair of shoes, an athame, a spell kit, and pollen for my familiar.

I could rush home, pick it—and her—up, and disappear again.

All it would cost me was everything I had built in the last four years.

"I need to think." I had to settle on an exit strategy if this went south. "Can you guys handle the store?"

"Weird that you should ask." Camber tilted her name tag toward me. "It says here I'm a manager."

"Whoa." Arden flashed hers at me. "I got one too." She dropped her mouth open. "We must have both put quarters in the same bubble gum machine."

"Maybe it was a misprint," I countered, "and your boss was too cheap to correct the problem."

"Then our boss really shouldn't have cut us both keys too." Camber shoved me toward the back. "Shoo."

"Go home," Arden urged me. "Take a bubble bath, drink some wine, and think about next steps."

Wine was the last thing I ought to reach for in this mood. I wouldn't stop chugging until I couldn't think.

Hmm.

Maybe she was on to something.

"Thanks." I grabbed my book then lingered on the threshold to the rear exit. "Call if you need me."

"We will," they chimed, lying through the perfectly straight teeth I helped finance.

Crossing to the shopping center's dedicated employee parking lot, I made it three steps before rock-hard arms encircled me, lifting me *way* too high and leaving my shoes dangling a foot above the pavement.

A scream lodged in my throat, and magic singed my tongue in a spell I could spit at my attacker, but there was a familiar weight to the careful hands linked at my navel. "Clay?"

Stones tumbled in his throat as he spun me toward him. "Miss me, Dollface?"

The smile cutting his rough-hewn lips forced mine into an unwilling curve to match.

"Nice rug." I rang my fingers through his short blond wig. "Still using Gorilla Glue?"

The unique texture of his skin required an industrial-strength bond to keep his hair in place.

"I had to look good for my best girl." His grin kept growing wider. "It's been too damn long."

"I just finished breakfast." I covered my mouth. "Maybe put me down if you don't want to wear it."

Seven feet tall. Four hundred pounds. Arms like tree trunks. I wasn't going anywhere unless he let me.

As a joke, he named himself Clayton Kerr when the Black Hats swore him in. He was a golem and molded from, well, clay. Ancient magic animated him, and enchantments gave him the look and feel of a human.

A *bald* human.

Beauty stores stocked fewer wigs than he rotated through during any given week.

Colors to match his every mood. Styles to fit any occasion. And their little travel boxes. So many boxes.

Vanity, thy name is Clayton Kerr.

That was before you factored in the company uniform, which was very Men in Black.

Expensive black suit, simple black tie, shiny black shoes, starched white dress shirt.

"Ace catch up to you yet?" He didn't release me. "He's not you, no one is, but he's a decent partner."

The unintentional dig slid between my ribs, right into my heart, but I had my reasons for going AWOL.

"He checked out my store, exploded the ovaries of my shopgirls, and left me his card."

"You hid from him?" Clay's eyes crinkled at the corners. *"You?"*

The power I once wielded stirred, blinking awake, rattling the chains I used to bind it within my skin.

But I was stronger than the hunger. I controlled it. It did *not* control me.

Anymore.

A roughness sanded the edges of my voice from the effort. "*Rue Hollis* hid from him."

"Rue is a white witch," he murmured, understanding what that meant. "How many years?"

"All of them." From the day I cut ties with Black Hat to this one. "Put me down, Clay."

"Not until you talk to Ace." Regret pinched his lips, but he didn't loosen his hold. "Director's orders."

Golems with Clay's agency were so rare as to be unheard of, which was how he ended up at Black Hat. Most of his kin were mindless dolls who followed instructions to the letter, but Clay had full autonomy until his free will smashed face-first into the brick wall that was a direct order from his current master.

By choice, he wouldn't hurt a fly, but he had done things under orders that twisted even my stomach. It shouldn't have been held against him, shouldn't have landed him in Black Hat, but he was only as moral as his current master allowed him to be.

"I understand." I bent as if to kiss his cheek but licked his forehead instead. "I'm sorry, Clay."

The magic animating him shorted out, his eyes clouded over, and he froze as solid as a statue.

The only way to best a golem was to smudge or erase the *shem*, one of the Names of God, written on his forehead. Any imperfections disrupted his flow of power, immobilizing him. And yes, they were all male.

Only someone he trusted would get anywhere near it, which made my betrayal cut both ways.

I broke his grip with a twist, hit the pavement with a grunt, then walked to my car with a slight limp.

Unless I wanted to run again, I had no choice but to retreat home, where I was safe.

Safer.

There were absolutes for people like me.

Black Hat's arrival in town had just proven that.

2

Gravel pinged the undercarriage of my sporty little crossover as I pulled into Mrs. Gleason's driveway. As much as I wanted to breeze past my closest neighbor and get home behind my wards that much faster, I couldn't pretend I didn't see her when she was brandishing a pink shotgun in the air to get my attention.

"Rue." She banged on the car window with the side of her fist. "*Rue.*"

As I lowered the glass, I reminded myself a gunshot wound probably wouldn't kill me. "Yes, ma'am?"

"The biggest man I ever did see was at your house." She stood on tiptoe with a hand as high as she could reach to give me an idea of height. "Don't you worry, darlin'." She squared her thin shoulders. "I run him off before he got any ideas."

Who could it have been but Clay? He probably laughed himself silly when she chased after him.

Mrs. Gleason was eighty pounds soaking wet, with a beehive hairdo that added a foot onto her height. A pair of house slippers snugged her tiny feet, and she wore a billowing snap-front dressing

gown in violet. I happened to know she owned decals to change the
color of her shotgun to match her outfit, which told me how riled she
must have been if she left her porch mismatched to accuse Clay of
trespassing.

"Thank you." Warmth spread through my chest. "I appreciate
you looking out for me."

Goodness wasn't innate to me. I started out mimicking people
who behaved in the way I wanted to act. I embraced *fake it 'til you
make it* as a template for the person I wanted to become. I still had
days when I felt plain fake, but moments like this gave me hope it
was more than pretend change, that I was doing it.

"Shot him right in his behind." She kissed the barrel of her gun.
"Bam-Bam never misses."

"You..." I swallowed a laugh, "...shot him?"

"Sure did." Her grin revealed a lack of dentures. "Let me tell you,
he ain't coming back no time soon."

The last time her teeth went missing, she called me for help, and
I found them stuck in an apple. She left the whole mess balanced on
the back porch rail after the dentures refused to pry loose of the fruit,
and forgot about them. A squirrel tried to run off with it when I got
there, but the teeth kept freaking it out.

As someone with a box of real human teeth rattling around
under my bed, I was in no position to judge.

"Oh, I almost forgot." I reached to the floorboard. "I mixed up
more of that tea you like."

The blend, according to its label, contained white willow bark,
holy basil, nettles, hyssop, cramp bark, California poppy, and citrus
peel in an Assam black tea base. The additives were a touch more
exotic.

And it worked wonders on her rheumatoid arthritis.

"God bless you." She pinched my cheek until it hurt. "How much
do I owe you?"

"I can't charge you after what you did for me today." I passed
over a week's supply. "You're my hero."

A flush stained her weathered cheeks as she accepted the gift with a grunt of thanks.

"I ought to go check and see if he left a note." I put the SUV in reverse. "See you later."

"I'll keep Bam-Bam out 'til you call me," she hollered as I backed down the road. "Be safe, hon."

A small miracle allowed me to skirt two more elderly neighbors I made time to chat with every few days. I missed that connection when I went too long between visits with them, but I had to get home.

On top of a gently rolling hill sat the small brick house I bought through an online auction, sight unseen. I sank as much into renovations as I did the initial payout, but it suited me. The two acres of grass, weeds, and wildflowers sprinkled with trees gave me a connection to the earth that soothed my ragged soul.

The first order of business was to check the wards, which hummed steadily, as always.

From what I could tell, Clay hadn't tested my protections. Then again, I hadn't been kind to unwanted guests in my previous incarnation. He hadn't known until I told him that I changed my diet, which meant no one else would guess either. That would keep me safer. For the time being.

Confident the house and land were secure, I called Mrs. Gleason and told her to stand down.

The front door swung open before I reached it, and a breathy voice murmured, "We had company."

"I heard." I eased into the darkened foyer. "They visited the store too."

"I only saw the one." Colby Timms, my familiar, cleared her throat. "He was your partner, back then."

"Clayton Kerr." I spotted her perched on the back of the sofa. "He won't hurt you."

The moth was the size of a house cat with white fuzz covering her abdomen and a wispy off-white mane. Pearlescent wings tucked close to her body, and her velvety legs were black with creamy, slipperlike feet. Though we had agreed the uppermost set would be deemed *hands* despite the lack of fingers.

"Who did he bring with him?"

"His new partner." I sank into the cushions beside her. "I haven't met him yet."

"Why are they here?" She climbed down onto my lap for snuggles. "Why can't they leave us alone?"

"I didn't talk to them long enough to find out what they want." I stroked her soft back. "Me, I imagine."

"Does this mean we're moving again?" Her antennae quivered, the hairs prickling. "I like it here."

"I like it here too, but if we want to stay, we'll have to talk to the agents. We'll have to fight for it."

"I'm not a baby," she grumbled, her wide black eyes narrowing on mine. "I can help."

"No." I smiled down at her. "You're not a baby." I tickled her side. "You're ten whole years old."

Or she had been, when she died. That was ten years ago. Technically, she was twenty.

"I can do magic and everything." She puffed up her downy fur. "I'm not great at it, but I will be."

"You're incredible for your age." I drew her closer in a loose hug. "I'm very proud of you."

"Do you have the clay man's number?"

"I do."

"Call him."

The phone in my hand weighed a thousand pounds, which made pressing the familiar digits a Herculean feat. Thumb hovering over the call button, I checked with Colby one last time. "Are you sure?"

In answer, she used one of her feet to initiate the call before I could chicken out. "Yep."

Clay answered on the first ring. "Kerr."

"Hey," I said awkwardly. "How are you feeling?"

"Less like a statue than I did an hour ago."

Like me, Clay's new partner would have been trained in how to reanimate him.

But I still felt guilty for incapacitating him.

"I heard you paid me a house call."

"That old biddy shot me in the ass." He chuckled. "Funniest damn thing I've ever seen."

"Mrs. Gleason takes care of me."

"I'm glad to hear it." His voice softened. "Did you call just to check on me or...?"

"I want to talk." I rested a hand on Colby for comfort. "You came here for a reason, and I want to hear it."

"We can be at your place in twenty minutes."

"I'll be waiting." I ended the call. "Goddess bless, what a mess."

"You mean *we*'ll be waiting." Colby fluttered her wings in annoyance. "I'm not hiding this time."

"How about we don't put all our cards on the table? You can be our ace in the hole."

"I'll never climb out of the hole if I let you don't stop putting me in it."

The kid was smart, and she was right, but she was also mine to protect.

"Once they know about you, I won't be able to hide you from them."

Their ignorance of her existence was the thin barrier keeping her safe.

"Good." A tiny growl laced her voice. "I want them to see me."

"I'll allow this only if you promise to do what I say, when I say it."

"Deal." Her wings picked up speed until she fluttered at my eye level. "I'm going to patrol."

"Stay inside the wards." I pointed a warning finger at her. "We don't know what we're up against yet."

After rolling her eyes at me, she zoomed out the window I cracked for her and began her rounds.

The sad thing about kids, even dead ones, is they have to grow up sometime.

By the time the black SUV—because of course Black Hats drove black SUVs—turned onto the drive, I was on the porch in a rocker with a cup of ice-cold sweet tea in one hand and the improbable shifter romance in the other. I had three days left to finish it before the weekly book club meeting, not that I expected to attend under the circumstances, but I was hooked now.

Colby was in stealth mode, as in she was hiding behind the chimney, high on the roof.

To set the stage, I finished reading the chapter I was on before glancing up from the page. "Gentlemen."

The simple happiness in Clay's smile twisted a knife of regret in my gut. I really did miss the big lug.

"Rue, this is Asa Montenegro." He handled introductions. "Ace, this is Rue Hollis."

On the last line, Clay winked at me, as if Asa wasn't fully aware it was an alias.

"It's a pleasure to meet you," Asa rumbled. "Clay says nothing but good things about you."

All I can say about setting eyes on Asa Montenegro for the first time was...

Goddess bless.

Had I not already been sitting, I worried my knees might have buckled. No wonder the girls had drooled over him. He was gorgeous. But then, beauty came with the predatory package. There was no finer lure than a pretty face, and his was breathtaking.

With Clay standing next to him, I pegged Asa at just shy of six feet. Lean muscle covered his frame, no amount of tailoring could conceal that, but he managed to hide his powerful body better than most. He wore his hair parted down the middle, in braids so long he could have tucked their ends into his waistband or even stuffed the tips in his pockets. An oval disc the color of moonlight hung from each ear, and a thick silver hoop pierced his septum.

The hair and the jewelry hinted at daemon heritage, but the sharpness of his features and his jewel-tone eyes, a bright peridot green, screamed fae.

A faint smile played around his full lips as he watched me cataloguing his features, as if he were used to enduring such inspections often and had decided to find the process amusing rather than insulting.

Embarrassed at being caught, I cut the niceties. "Why are you here?"

"The director wants you to consult on a case," Clay answered for them. "We need an expert on…"

"…black magic," I finished for him. "You can say it."

There was no changing my past or anyone else's. All we could do was live with the consequences.

"Four girls are missing." Asa spun a silver ring on his finger. "We need your help finding their killer."

"You said *missing*." Rustling drew my attention to the roof, but I kept my eyes forward. "I don't follow."

"Eight other girls have gone missing. Each time, they were taken in groups of four."

"Their bodies were found one month after their abductions." Clay worked his jaw. "They were *left* for us to find. The killer wanted to make sure his work didn't go unnoticed."

A tendril of magic unfurled within me, hungry for what they offered after living on so little for so long.

"There are other witches you could contact." I sipped my tea, tasting ashes of the past. "Why me?"

"There are similarities to a case you worked with Clay." Asa quit his fidgeting. "We think we're dealing with a copycat."

Bile rose up my throat, and I washed it down with more sugar that didn't help. "Which case?"

Clay smoothed a hand over his head. "The Silver Stag."

"*No.*"

The men jerked to attention, and I shut my eyes, wishing I hadn't agreed to Colby's demands.

"He's dead." The moth charged them in a rush of fury. "Rue killed him and ate his heart. I *saw* it."

The rocker creaked as I stood, my heart breaking for her. "Colby..."

"They're wrong." She darted as close to them as she dared without crossing the ward. "You're wrong."

While my former partner blanched as if he had seen a ghost, and he had, Asa hit his knees. In his suit. It must have cost a small fortune, yet he hadn't hesitated. Not for a second. He bowed his head, rested his palms flat on his thighs, and murmured a soft prayer.

"You're Colby Timms," Clay said softly, a world of understanding in his coarse voice.

The last of the Silver Stag's victims. A fae girl who had turned ten the night before she was taken.

It had always struck me as ironic they named him the Silver *Stag* when he had a preference for does.

"You kept her." Asa's tone chilled me to the bone. "All this time."

I jerked my chin up a notch. "I did."

"You captured a loinnir...a sacred being...a *child*...for food."

The comic shock on Clay's face when he registered his partner's words almost made me laugh.

"Yes." I crossed my arms over my chest. "How did you think I was so powerful, daemon?"

The heat in my words caused Clay to drag a hand down his face. "Shit."

"That's why I ran." I aimed my rant toward Asa, who had yet to rise. "I saw an opportunity for power, and I took it. Happy? Now you get to feel righteous when you watch me burn for my crimes."

"Burn?" Colby squeaked. "He's going to *burn* you?"

"I'm a witch," I said flatly. "What am I but kindling?"

The moth spun midair, raced to me, and hit me hard enough to knock me back into the rocker.

"I was wrong," she sobbed. "I don't want to fight. I want to run. Let's go. Let's just go. Please?"

Cradling her against my chest, I petted and soothed her. "I shouldn't have said that."

"They can't hurt you." She clung to my shirt in six places. "I won't let them."

"Do you understand what she's doing to you?" Asa's glare cut like a razor. "She's feeding on you."

"Do you understand anything?" Colby twisted in my arms. "She *saved* me."

"Let's all take a breath." Clay held up his hands. "Ace, dial it down, man."

"I won't allow this." He rose in a fluid motion. "It goes against everything I believe in."

His ripe disgust was nothing I hadn't felt toward myself, but his condemnation slid off me this time.

I might not have done the right thing by Colby, but I had done what my conscience demanded of me.

Wings jittering with agitation, Colby puffed up her fur. "You don't get a say."

"Little one, you don't understand." He placed a hand over his heart. "I can help you find peace."

Peace was code for exorcising her spirit, her *self*, into whatever afterlife awaited her.

"Go inside and play your game." I bent down to kiss the top of her head. "Please?"

Antennae quivering, bristling like bottle brushes, she growled, "I'm old enough to—"

"For me?"

"You owe me a new mount for this." She twitched her butt at the agents then flew back in. "A *dragon*."

That would set me back twenty-five dollars, but it was worth it to buy a moment alone with these two.

Rising from my chair, I descended the steps slowly to give the rage burning in my black heart time to cool.

The wards hummed as I neared them, but I had no intention of crossing the barrier and putting Colby at risk of capture. I stopped in front of Asa, rested my hands on the white picket fence, and let the claws at my fingertips extend into the wood to prevent me from raking them across his handsome face.

"The Silver Stag murdered that little girl." I pitched my voice low. "She was his last victim." I took a deep breath. "As he lay dying at my feet, he called her soul from her body and wrapped her in the form you just saw." A creature unlike any in this world. "He chose a moth so he could summon her. He would have ordered her to fly to her own death at his command. He planned to consume her to heal himself, as if her essence was a fluff of cotton candy for him to pop into his mouth until it dissolved on his tongue."

"I didn't know." Clay wiped a hand over his mouth. "You never said…"

"Your partner here thinks I kept Colby as a snack." I mimed a casual shrug. "I can't blame him." I told him the truth. "I would think the worst of someone with my reputation too." I held his gaze. "It's earned."

A tilt of his head transformed Asa's aggression into curiosity. "Why did you resist?"

"She was afraid," I rasped, a hole opening in my chest. "So very afraid." I retracted my claws. "I killed the Silver Stag, but his spell was draining her. A soul can't survive outside its shell for long. She was dying all over again. Slowly. Painfully. As she clawed at any means to hold on to life." I couldn't look at either of them. "Even now, I hear those screams in my dreams."

They reminded me so much of how I had sounded, begging for mercy as a child after…

"You took her as your familiar." Clay understood first. "You bound her to you to save her."

The link to me gave her substance, allowed her to become *real*, but it also trapped her as a moth.

"I did." I rubbed my arms against a chill. "She was a child then, and she's a child now."

That moment of weakness, of compassion, might have been the culmination of my darkest act yet.

A familiar mingled its life force with its witch. That was why it was taboo to bond with a child. They quit aging, physically. They were fixed for the rest of their lives—and witches lived for a *long* time—at the exact developmental point in which the link was forged. The bond that saved Colby locked her mental age too.

For as long as we both lived, Colby would be a child in my care, and that was an enormous responsibility.

One I would happily take on all over again for the chance to learn what it was to love another person.

Even if she was, well, an insect.

"She can't function as a proper familiar." Asa dipped his chin. "You knew, and you did it anyway."

The pinch in Clay's brows eased a fraction. "That's why you went white."

"A girl killed by black magic shouldn't have to live with someone who practices it."

"I owe you an apology." Asa bowed his head in a show of respect. "I shouldn't have assumed—"

"I left Black Hat." I stood my ground. "I'm not going back."

"You would let more children die?" Asa slid his gaze past my shoulder. "Can you live with that?"

"More children like Colby." I filled in the blanks for him. "That's what you mean."

The appeal to my better nature would have been laughable a decade earlier. Now I was...softer.

"I can't go back." I stared at the ground as if the right answers might sprout. "I can't risk Colby."

Black Hat might have found me, but Colby had gobsmacked Clay and Asa, which meant she was still a secret.

"We need your expertise on this case." Asa took a step away. "Will you sleep on it?"

"It won't change my answer," I warned him. "I have to do what's best for Colby."

"I understand." He made a gesture at the level of his navel. "Until tomorrow, Rue Hollis."

Backing away from the fence, he pivoted on his heel then returned to the SUV.

"I wish you had told me." Clay stuck his hands in his pockets. "I could have helped you."

Because this was Clay, I could admit, "I was afraid I was no better than your partner thinks I am."

Had I consumed Colby, I would have rocketed from sixth or seventh most powerful black witch in the country straight to the top. My kind ate hearts to gain power, but to devour a soul? A *pure* soul? The high would have sustained me for decades and left its mark on my magic for the rest of my long life.

"You never harmed innocents." He lifted his hand as if to comfort me before recalling the wards. "You're one of the good ones."

"I'm a serial killer who hunts—*hunted*—worse monsters."

That I had preyed on the guilty didn't make me an angel of mercy, merely an opportunist.

"Sometimes, that's what it takes." His lips quirked to one side. "You did good with the kid. She's fierce."

"Colby is the same person she was when she died." I shook my head. "I can't take credit."

That belonged to her parents, to her. And for the second time in my life, I heard a whisper of conscience.

The Silver Stag was dead, his victims avenged. I ended my career on a high note. I had nothing to prove.

But Asa had done his job well. He had planted a bug in my ear that forced me to ask *what if.*

What if there were more Colbys out there? *What if* I could save them? *What if* I was the only one who could?

"I'll talk to Colby." I bet she had been eavesdropping. "We'll meet you for breakfast with an answer."

"Text me the details?"

"I can't believe you kept the same number."

"I was only ever a phone call away, Dollface. That won't change."

Throat squeezing shut, I lifted a hand in a wave then returned to the porch, balancing the weight of the world on my shoulders.

3

I wore Colby as a hair bow to our breakfast meeting with Clay and Asa.

Whatever her type of otherworldly moth, they came in two sizes. Regular and mini. Or maybe that was a familiar thing. Either way, I wasn't about to look a gift moth in the mouth. With her neutral coloring, she matched everything, and I often passed her off as an accessory when she wanted to go to town with me.

The door opened before I touched it as Ms. Hampshire yanked me into her diner and into a hug.

"Frank has been right as rain since he started drinking your tea." She kissed both my cheeks. "Bless you."

Based on Mrs. Gleason's glowing reviews of her tea blend, Ms. Hampshire had approached me about holistic cures for her partner's emphysema. His label read: elderberry, eucalyptus, lemon peel, chickweed, holy basil, pleurisy root, and spearmint. The other ingredients, well, they were best left unlisted.

"I'm happy to help." I withdrew. "I'm meeting someone this morning. Two someones, actually."

"I know the pair you're meaning." Her brow creased. "Never seen the likes of them around here."

"They're police officers." I stuck to my fabricated backstory. "They helped with my ex and my new identity."

"Why are they here?" She slapped her order pad against her palm. "Has there been any trouble?"

"No." I hit her with a bright smile as fake as my name. "Nothing like that."

"All right." She cut her eyes toward them. "I trust the big one more than the pretty one."

Supernaturals, having excellent hearing, would have no trouble picking up on our conversation.

Ms. Hampshire's comment drew Asa's attention to me, as if he was curious how I would answer.

There was fae in his lineage. No doubt about it. Fae vanity was legendary.

"You think he's pretty?" I swept my gaze over him. "I didn't notice."

"Sure." She ribbed me with her elbow. "I didn't notice the sky is blue or the grass is green either."

"Call the shop when you're ready for a refill." I couldn't help my smile. "The girls will let me know."

"I'll do that." She patted my cheek. "Breakfast is on me." She hesitated. "Yours." She shot Clay a furtive glance. "Feeding that one would cost me the earth."

"That's not necessary," I said over a laugh, "but thank you."

"Don't go looking for your check," she warned. "You won't find it."

"Yes, ma'am."

"Oh, before I forget." She touched the side of her head. "That's a lovely hairclip you're wearing."

"Thanks." I stroked a finger down Colby's back. "I think so too."

"That tickles," the moth hissed. "Stop it."

The urge to squirm overwhelmed her, and she dug her feet into my scalp, which only made me laugh.

Crossing the restaurant, I joined the agents at their booth, grateful they had squished in together to give me my own bench.

"Good morning, gentlemen."

The cushions squeaked under me as I slid across them to the middle for a clear view of them both.

"Morning, Dollface." Clay's smile couldn't grow any bigger. "Damn, it's good to see you."

A harsh intake of breath on top of my head caused the big man to blush clear to the roots of his wig.

Today he had chosen a conservative style, by his standards, brown with blond streaks in a messy cut.

"He said a bad word," Colby whispered, delighted. "Rue won't let me say bad words."

"I apologize." Clay winced. "I shouldn't say bad words either."

"You're old." Her wings twitched in a shrug. "You can say whatever you want."

Flattened against the wall by Clay's bulk, Asa fought a smile. "What will you have for breakfast?"

Out of necessity, Colby kept her social life online. It took her a second to register he was talking to her.

"I ate before we left." She stomped my head. "Don't forget, you promised me hot chocolate."

"With extra marshmallows." I rolled my eyes. "I haven't forgotten."

Before we got down to business, Ms. Hampshire bustled over to take our orders.

Unsurprising, Clay ordered more food than we had room at the table, which worked, since Asa only ordered a black coffee. I went with bacon and pancakes, their daily special, and an orange juice.

"I'll get that hot chocolate out to you in a minute," she promised. "I have to find the marshmallows."

This time of year, this far south, I doubted many orders came through for hot chocolate when it was iced sweet tea weather. But she always made a point to keep the supplies on hand for *my* cravings.

Thankfully, it held up well on the ride home, the only place Colby could enjoy her treat.

Once we were alone again, I pressed my palms onto the table to hide their trembling. "I'm in."

"We're in," my hair bow informed them. "We're a team."

"In exchange for my—*our* assistance—I request that the Bureau drafts me a new contract that specifies I will only work for Black Hat on a case-by-case basis as a consultant. This town will be my permanent address, until such time Colby and I decide we no longer wish to live here. We expect to be left in peace, barring necessary communications that pertain to potential cases." I aimed my stare at Asa. "I have a business to run and obligations to this community. Our demands are nonnegotiable."

They had their hooks in me, and we all knew it, but maybe I could determine how deep the barbed edge pierced this new life of mine.

"We don't have the authority to approve or deny your request, but we'll hand it upline and see what the director has to say." Asa rubbed his thumb in the bowl of his spoon. "Perhaps by tonight." He studied his reflection. "Will you have dinner with me? As an apology for my earlier rudeness?"

"Like a date?" Colby tap-danced on my head. "Rue *never* dates."

The agent lifted his piercing green eyes to mine. "Is that so?"

"He meant the four of us." I ignored his question, and her excitement. "A business dinner."

"I'm leaving after breakfast." Clay cut Asa epic side-eye. "I won't be back until tomorrow."

"I have to study," Colby said primly. "I'm working toward my GED."

"Impressive." Clay's eyebrows climbed up his forehead. "I don't have one of those."

"I want to go to college." Her tone dared them to tell her she couldn't do it. "I want to be a lawyer."

"There are educational grants available to Black Hat agents and their families." Asa regarded her seriously. "They might be able to help Rue offset those costs."

"No thanks." I wasn't allowing them that much access to Colby. "I'm happy to pay out of pocket."

Her attention span was impressive, considering her mental age, but she bounced around a lot, as all kids do. Last week, she wanted to be a vet. This week, a lawyer. Next week, who knew? All that mattered to me was she believed she could do anything she set her mind to, wherever that road took her.

"Here you go." Ms. Hampshire appeared with two other girls in tow. "Breakfast is served."

"Thank you." I salivated over my stack of pancakes swimming in syrup. "We appreciate the fast service."

"It would have been quicker if your friend here hadn't ordered half the contents of my fridge." Her laugh was bright and warm. "Frank thought we must have gotten a school bus of fieldtrippers in."

"I took a good look at everyone else's plates on my way in." Clay dialed up his charm. "Everything looked so good, I couldn't choose just one thing. I had to sample it all."

"Oh, you." A bright flush lit up her cheeks. "Watch yourself around this one."

With his simple coffee, Asa watched our byplay as if it were a better meal than what sat on the table.

"Well, I'll let you get back to your visiting." She pinched my cheek. "Holler if you need anything."

Once she was out of sight, I rubbed the tender skin, which was sore from an excess of pinches.

That was the problem with eternal youth. I could pass for mid-twenties, though I was probably her age. I had kept the round cheeks of my childhood, and their always flushed appearance made them irresistible to grandmotherly types. Pair that with wide blue eyes and wheat-colored waves that hit me mid-spine, and I could pass for a kid fresh out of high school.

The camouflage had served me well, and make no mistake, it was camouflage. Nothing about me had been left to nature or to chance. I was the culmination of generations of selective breeding that resulted in power, beauty, and intelligence wrapped up in one girl-next-door package.

I was brittle black and charred inside, with a charcoal briquet for a heart. How no one saw it shocked me until working for the Black Hats taught me that most people only saw what you showed them.

Out of safe topics of conversation, I veered toward the dicey. "How is everyone else?"

"The same." Clay dug into his bacon, egg, and cheese sandwich. "Immortals don't change much."

"True." I picked at my pancakes with my fork. "Days, weeks, months, years blur in the office."

Black Hat didn't hire its agents. It blackmailed, kidnapped, bought, stole, traded, or threatened them.

"Ace is the only newbie," he continued. "He's been with us...eight years?"

"Seven." Asa sipped his coffee. "How long until I'm no longer the newbie?"

"Until we get another newbie." Clay bit down with gusto. "Probably another decade or three."

Asa studied me over the rim of his mug. "How long were you the newbie?"

"Five years." I set down my fork. "One of our agents went rogue, and Clay and I hunted him down."

We killed him when he resisted arrest using deadly force. I picked his heart out of my teeth for days.

"She was promoted on a technicality." Clay sucked on his teeth. "Some newbs have all the luck." His eyes laughed at me. "Makes me sick."

It made me sick too, the reminder of that first kill on the job.

"Are you going to eat that?"

Jerked from my grim thoughts, I found Asa staring at me. "You want my pancakes?"

"They look good." He turned the mug in his hand. "You're not eating them."

"I seem to have lost my appetite." I pushed the plate over to him. "Please, help yourself."

A piece of egg fell out of Clay's open mouth as he watched Asa settle in with my food.

Eyebrows on the rise, I invited him to inform me what the big deal was, but he got back to chewing.

"There you are," a warbly voice called across the restaurant. "Hey, darlin'."

An elderly man with dark skin shining with sweat toddled over with a twinkle in his eyes.

"Oh no." I covered my face with my hands and pretended to hide. "Not this guy."

"Hey, now. Hey. We're friends, right?" He cackled with delight. "How you been?"

Lowering my hands before the agents got the wrong idea, I smiled up at Old Man Jenkins. "Good. You?"

"Not dead yet." He reached in a pocket and pulled out a glass bottle. "You cured me."

The tincture blended elderberry, horehound, ginger root, cinnamon stick, and star anise.

A tasty cure for the common cold. No magic required.

"Let me know if you need more." I curled his hand over the bottle. "I keep plenty on hand."

"You're too good to me." He staggered back, noticing the agents. "Hey, now. Hey. Who are you?"

"They're friends." I indicated the mountain of food. "They're just passing through."

"Hmph." He narrowed his rheumy eyes at Asa and then Clay. "You best treat her right."

Unable to help myself, I leaned closer. "Mrs. Gleason shot Clay here in the butt."

"Ha." He slapped his thigh. "God love that woman. God love you too, Miss Hollis."

Laughing under his breath, he shuffle-stepped off to his usual table with a wide grin.

Crunching through a piece of bacon, Clay chewed thoughtfully. "Your friend didn't ask about my health."

"You're here, sitting and eating. As far as he's concerned, that means you're fine."

"You haven't accepted payment for any of the teas or tinctures you've given to your neighbors."

Leave it to Asa to notice. "How would you know?"

Without answering, he dipped his chin and took a bite of my pancakes.

"How do you earn a living?" Clay shoved a blueberry muffin in his mouth. "This town is itty-bitty."

"I hunt unicorns under the full moon, saw off their horns, and grind them to powder I sell online."

As far as hair bows go, Colby giggle-snorted way too much to pass for the real thing.

"Her store." Asa bit into my bacon while holding my gaze. "It's remarkable."

The natural redness in my cheeks kept my blush from showing, but I got the sense he read me just fine.

"Believe it or not, the apothecary pulls its own weight. Lotions, hand soaps, bodywashes, lip balms. Teas, oils, tinctures, poultices. All made using family recipes that are at least as old as you are, Clay." I sipped a little OJ. "I might employ the use of secret ingredients here and there, but I do no harm."

A shift of Clay's hips as he located his cell caused his side of the booth to groan for mercy.

"Dam—" He bit off the curse with a blush. "*Darn* it." He threw money on the table. "I have to go."

"Have fun." I added enough cash to cover my meal plus a tip. "Try not to get shot." I smiled. "Again."

Asa picked my contribution off the pile, pushed the folded bills back to me, then added his own.

Uncertain what was happening, I broke down and asked him, "What are you doing?"

"I ate the food." He indicated his clean plate. "The least I can do is pay for it."

"As I'm sure you heard, my meal was on the house."

"Yet you paid."

"Well...yes." I shoved the money back. "I don't like taking advantage of people."

"Neither do I."

"See you tomorrow." Clay chucked me under my chin. "Have I mentioned how good it is to see you?"

"Only every five minutes since you accosted me outside my shop."

"I'm sorry about that." His gaze dipped to the floor. "You know how it is."

"I do." I kicked his shin under the table. "I don't hold it against you."

"Later, ladies." He waved a big hand. "And yes, I included you in that, Ace."

"Keep me updated," his partner warned. "Routine transports can go sideways fast."

"A transport?" I swirled my OJ. "Now that I know I'm part of a twofer, I feel less special."

"The transport is cover to explain why we're here without alerting anyone to your location."

"What he said." Clay took one last swig of his coffee. "We're doing our best to fly under the radar."

"Who sent you?" I set down my glass. "Specifically?"

"The director." Clay left it at that. "Personally."

The director had a vested interest in me. I had zero interest in him. But I wasn't surprised to hear he had bided his time until he could use a copycat killer, a fact I had yet to verify, to lure me back into the fold.

"Email me copies of the case files." Involvement from the director changed things. "I checked last night, and my work email is still good." The director knew my location, so there were no worries about him using my login to find me. "Send it there."

Aside from the usual Bureau junk that clogged everyone's inboxes, I discovered a mountain of email Clay had sent me over the years. The tone of the first one, sent a week after I disappeared, ripped my heart out through my nose. I couldn't finish reading it, and I couldn't bear to open the others. Deleting them was out of the question, so I filed them away.

The way Clay rubbed the base of his neck told me he was thinking about those emails too.

"I'll have to clear it with the director," Asa said. "Until your other request is approved or denied, we have to treat you as a rogue agent, and that means no sharing sensitive details of an ongoing investigation."

"I understand." I cut my eyes toward Clay, whose poker face was nonexistent. "I look forward to hearing from you."

Trailing a finger across his forehead, he turned and left with a smile for the proprietress.

Asa rested his elbows on the table. "What did he mean by that?"

"Are you serious?" I snorted a laugh then realized he meant it. "Oh." I cleared my throat. "He was asking if he's got *sucker* stamped on his forehead."

"You two read each other well."

"We were partners for a long time."

Thirty years, give or take. A blip in time for him. A lifetime for me.

"I've never seen Clay so animated."

Given my earlier faux pas, I verified, "Was that a joke?"

"Yes."

"It was a good one." I allowed myself a laugh. "Tell Clay the next time you talk. He'll love it."

"I'll do that." He rested his chin on his fist. "You aren't what I expected."

"Yes, well, I'm still evil deep down where it counts." I scooted down the bench. "I've also got to go."

"Because Clay left."

"Because I have a store that opens in fifteen minutes."

"Ask him about dinner," a tiny voice coaxed from my hair.

"Asa—" A frown pinched my lips when he shut his eyes. "Are you okay over there?"

"Yes." His eyes, when he opened them, were as black as I imagined my soul to be. "I'm fine."

"Maybe dinner isn't a good idea." I shifted my body to shield other diners from him. "Your eyes are..."

"Apologies." He lowered his head. "I'll text you about dinner."

"You have my number?"

From this angle, I caught a hint of his smile. "It is printed on your business cards, yes."

Laughter spilled down from the top of my head, which drew his dark gaze up to Colby.

I had been wrong, I realized. His eyes weren't black. They were a crimson so deep as to be fathomless.

And he had caught me staring at him again.

Dinner with Asa was a bad idea.

Too bad those were my specialty.

4

As much as I would have loved to drive Colby home before heading in to work, especially with Black Hat scrutinizing me, I needed to see Camber and Arden to reassure them I was okay after yesterday's drama.

With a social circle of one, Colby lived for *take your moth to work* days.

A chorus of haunted moans greeted me when I pushed into the store.

"Welcome to..." Camber glanced up from behind the counter. *"Rue."*

"Rue?" Arden shot out from the back room. "You're here."

Hand behind my back, I twisted the lock and the sign to give us a moment alone.

"We need to talk." I examined the sidewalk through the glass but saw only locals. "Let's go in the back."

The back room was my office, the supply closet, and our workspace all crammed into one.

Three of us barely fit without bumping elbows, which would have been fine if they weren't spitting mad.

"I thought we agreed you would stay home." Camber tapped her foot. "Why are you here?"

"I agreed to *consider* staying home."

"You freaked when that guy came in yesterday." Arden folded her arms. "Why aren't you freaked now?"

This was the worst part, having to tap-dance around the truth to keep them safe from my world.

"The guy who came into the store wasn't the ex." I had to temper this lie with facts to smooth the lumps I had created in my story. "I was shocked when I heard his voice, and I flew into panic mode." That much was one hundred percent real. "I let you guys think the worst, and I'm sorry for that."

The harsh frowns knitting their foreheads eased a fraction as they absorbed what I was telling them.

"Who was he then?" Camber's scowl cut deep. "Why was he looking for you?"

"He's one of the cops who handled my case." I kept to the mental script I'd recited for Ms. Hampshire. "He heard my ex was in the area and came with his partner to warn me."

"Why not call you?" Arden drummed her fingers on her elbows. "Why drop in without warning?"

They were not making this easy. It warmed my heart. But it also had me breaking a sweat.

"I changed my number." I was honest there. "I stopped checking my old email address."

"How did they find you?" Camber quit tapping her foot. "It was the store, wasn't it?"

"It wasn't the store." I wouldn't let them shoulder that blame. "It was my tax returns."

Okay, so most paras didn't pay taxes. We paid tithes to our covens, packs, clans, prides, etc.

A bucket of doubt dumped over Camber. "You used your home address?"

"I used a business mailing service that gave me a physical

address, which was their store. Then I paid the fee to have my mail forwarded. Rinse and repeat seven times, with each address in a different state. The last stop is my post office box here in town."

"They staked out the post office." Arden pulled on her bottom lip. "I saw that on *True Crimes* once."

"Maybe." I had to get out the rest. "They want me to help them put my ex away for good."

The girls reached for me, each one taking a hand. Their palms were sweaty, and their hearts beat loud.

A bare whisper passed Arden's lips. "Are you going to do it?"

"Can they keep you safe?" Camber squeezed hard. "Don't risk it if they can't protect you."

"I owe it to any future victims to try." That much was the truth. "Nothing is decided yet."

"You're considering it, though." Camber straightened her shoulders. "We can take care of the store."

"That's what you mean." Arden clued in after her friend. "You're going away."

"Not forever." I dropped their hands and pulled them in for a hug. "Not for long, I hope."

"We'll support your decision," Camber vowed. "We can bring in Gran to help if we need extra hands."

Miss Dotha wasn't a witch, but she and Camber came from them. So did Arden's people for that matter.

The girls were human, but that drop or two of distant witch blood made them compatible with what our store made and sold. Miss Dotha wasn't interested in a full-time job, but she pitched in when I left town.

Every year, I closed shop for a whole week to take Colby somewhere new. Vacations were new for me—it wasn't a thing my family had ever done—and I had grown to love our annual girls-only adventure.

"I would appreciate that." I turned them loose. "I'll let you know what I decide."

"You can count on us." Arden found her smile. "We've got your back."

A grin curving her lips, Camber leaned in. "Does this mean the scorching hot guy *isn't* bad news?"

"I didn't say that." I wasn't sure what to think of him. "Plus, he's too old for you."

With his heritage, he was likely near or past the century mark. For him to have attracted the attention of Black Hat, and gotten *recruited*, he must be powerful...and dangerous. Agents fit a certain, lethal profile.

"Age is just a number," she countered. "I'm legal."

"Nineteen is *barely* legal."

"I'll be twenty in three months."

"He'll be gone tomorrow."

A knock on the front door sent Arden scurrying to answer, figuring it must be one of our regulars.

Not five seconds later, she scurried right back, hiccupping so hard she couldn't get out the message.

"He's baaack," Camber teased. "Are you sure I can't have him?"

"Ask your gran that." I bared my teeth at her. "I dare you."

Anyone who knew my history would have shivered at the display, but these girls only saw a smile.

"I better go see what he wants." A half hour between visits was borderline stalking. "Be right back."

On my way to the front, I enjoyed the view far too much. I wished I could blame the uptick of my breath on the cloud of teen girl pheromones I left in the office, but I worried the warmth in my belly was on me.

Yet another downside to my cover story. Men in town either revered me like the Virgin Mary for my past or avoided me like my emotional baggage might leap into their trunk if they so much as smiled at me.

For the most part, it was a good thing. Celibacy kept men out of my house and out of my life.

Our lives.

I didn't want a relationship, and vibrators made choosing the perfect man easier than going around asking for a peek in your date's pants before you made it to the restaurant.

But the fact I was now wondering about the fit of Asa's pants was a bad sign.

Maybe I had been around humans for too long if the first para to cross my path melted my panties.

Asa made no move to enter the store, so I joined him on the sidewalk. "Forget something?"

"Clay called." He rolled up his shirtsleeves, which struck me as somehow obscene. "He's in trouble."

I was too.

Forearms were *not* an erogenous zone.

"Oh no," the tiny voice from my hair squeaked. "What happened?"

Never in my life had I been more grateful Colby and I didn't share a mental bond, as some familiars did with their practitioners. Here I was, mentally shopping for Asa-inspired vibrators, and I forgot about her.

Oh, yeah.

This was bad.

"What she said." I recovered my mental dignity. "What's wrong?"

"He was sent to collect a young dryad." His gaze drifted up to Colby's perch. "She's resisting arrest."

Poor Clay wouldn't hurt a leaf on her head. "And you're telling me this...why?"

"The agent he was providing backup for is..." he pursed his lips, "...napping under a tree."

One thing Black Hat drummed into its agents was to always, always stick with your partner on a call.

"Why doesn't Clay wake them up?" Colby wanted to know. "He needs someone to watch his back."

"I agree." Asa slid his gaze to mine. "I was hoping Rue would go with me to help him."

This had the smell of a trap all over it, but I couldn't fault his ploy. Clay was a huge soft spot for me.

"She will," Colby volunteered me then tiptoed forward to peer down at me. "I like Clay."

Figuring I could nip this rebellion in the bud, I told him, "I'll have to drop Colby off at home first."

"That's okay." She tapped my forehead. "I have to meet my friends for a raid anyhow."

Asa's eyebrows rose. "A raid?"

"I play a lot of Mystic Realms." She sighed at his blank expression. "It's an MMRPG."

Brackets formed to either side of his lips as he pondered her meaning.

"A massively multiplayer online role-playing game?"

Poor Asa was still drawing a blank, so I intervened before Colby recruited him for her guild.

"A girl's gotta socialize." I wiggled my brows to drive Colby back into place. "I can barely keep her avatar, and its adorable pet, straight, but she knows *everyone*. It sounds like a wild party in my living room every night."

Understanding darkened his eyes, and he dipped his chin. "Maybe you can show me sometime."

"Sure." Her little feet tickled my scalp. "I like helping newbs."

Asa lifted his eyes to mine, a pleat across his brow, which almost made up for his wrangling an invitation into my house.

"Newbies," I explained. "People who are new to the game."

"Ah." He swept his gaze over my face. "Will you join me?"

For a second, I got my wires crossed. "In the game?"

I had an avatar, but she had died horribly so many times, I elected to let her rest in peace.

"He meant help with Clay." Colby snuggled in. "She will."

"Excellent." Asa awarded her a smile that hitched my breath. "Can I give you a ride home?"

"I need to run a few errands first." I checked the time. "Meet me at my house in thirty minutes."

"I'll be there."

With one hand in his pocket, he strolled the sidewalk until a store caught his interest and he went in.

"You're grounded," I told my naughty hair bow. "Grounded into the dirt."

"You have zero follow through." She scoffed at my tone. "You just like to make threats."

Who had I become that a tiny moth sassed me without fear of the consequences?

Probably a better person.

But could a better person stop a copycat when the original Silver Stag had nearly beaten my worst?

Camber and Arden shared way too many knowing glances for my comfort when I made my excuses.

I refused to believe I was so hard up for a man that everyone felt matchmaking was my only hope.

Dry spells happened to everyone. A decade wasn't that long, right? Or two? Had it already been three?

By the time I set Colby up with her bee pollen granules and sugar water, I was ready to escape her smug—if adorably so—face too. Her little headset slayed me with its cuteness. Her whole gaming setup was built to spec for her comfort, since virtual friends were the easiest for her to manage.

Well, real friends. Virtual landscape. Pixels didn't exchange Christmas presents, you know?

With her settled in for her raid, I checked to make sure I had all my supplies.

Jeans, boots, tee, spell kit, and athame. The spell kit reminded me of a jumbo leather fanny pack, except it buckled like a belt at my waist then fastened around my upper thigh to provide extra stability for vials. The overall effect was very steampunkish, but it was an heirloom piece, and its weight comforted me.

"I'll check in if we run late," I called on my way to the front door. "Have fun."

There was no answer, which wasn't unusual. She lived in those noise-cancelling headphones.

Best investment ever? Maybe. Though possibly the worst. It depended on the day and how loud I had to scream to get her attention. She suffered from bouts of selective hearing during school and chore times.

A parent might worry Colby was too plugged in for her own good, but I wasn't her mom. I was more like the fun aunt, the one who fed her niece too much sugar, bought her too many expensive toys, and let her stay up too late. I was just grateful technology had reached a point where she could experience any sort of normalcy to count the hours she spent glued to her computer screen.

Standing a good foot away from the white picket fence, Asa waited for me with a smoothie in hand.

"The man at the counter told me this was your usual." He offered it to me when I joined him outside the wards. "After quizzing me on how I knew you, what my intentions were, and when I was leaving."

"Thanks." I accepted the bribe, a godsend since I didn't eat at breakfast. "And don't take it personally."

"It's not just me?"

"Barry still asks me when I'm going back where I came from. I thought it meant he wanted me gone, but his wife assured me it's his way." I took a sip and had to admit, Asa was sly. "These things have too much sugar to qualify as healthy, but I do love a good strawberry, banana, pineapple smoothie."

We got in the SUV, which smelled of earthy tobacco and apples, and I spotted his pink drink.

"I wasn't sure what to try, so I got the same as you."

"What did you think?" I checked the fill line. "Have you tried it yet?"

"It's very sweet." He cranked the engine and started toward the main road. "The cold bothers me."

"Daemons prefer scalding coffee as black as damned souls?"

While he had ordered a cuppa Joe for breakfast, it also served as a dig about how others viewed his kind as Hell-dwelling, fire-pit-bathing, virgin-sacrificing, soul-eating minions of a red-pajama-clad dude named Satan.

Okay, so maybe I was still a *smidge* bitter his first impression of me was I kept Colby around as a snack.

"I ought to know better than to judge based on race, caste, or religion." He paused. "I apologize."

Gender and sexuality tended to be more flexible with long-lived beings, but he nailed the sticking points.

"You did come on strong." I set my drink in the empty holder. "Not that I blame you."

I had earned my reputation. He was right to believe the worst of me. I would have in his place.

"I shouldn't have been so quick to accuse you. Daemons have their own reputation to overcome."

Like they weren't demons. Demons weren't real. Or that they came from Hell. Hell didn't exit. Hael did.

"We don't have to kiss and make up." I stared out the window. "This is one job, not a partnership."

"Things will go smoother if we get along."

"Does Clay actually need help? Or did you lure me away for the chance to smooth things over?"

"The agent Clay went to back up was crushed to death by the dryad. She beat her to a pulp."

"Did you hear that pop?" I faked searching the cab. "I think that was the sound of my ego deflating."

Subtle tension clenched his fingers where they gripped the

wheel. "Did you want me to get you alone?"

Reaching for my drink, I pulled up short. "Did you want me to want you to get me alone?"

The two cups were identical, so were their contents. Only their fullness levels had distinguished them.

As I tended to gulp down my breakfast of choice, I expected to be slurping air, but there was plenty left.

That was odd, but I had been paying more attention to him than my drink, so maybe I miscalculated?

Just because he ate my pancakes *after* I passed on them didn't mean he switched our drinks. "No."

The inner debate over my sanity lent my voice an undecided quality, which earned me a thoughtful look.

This was ridiculous. There was nothing hinky going on here. But...was that a dare glinting in his eyes?

Picking up the drink from the holder nearest to me, I took a cautious sip, barely enough to taste.

When that didn't kill me, I held a big gulp on my tongue, letting it dissolve as I waited for any weirdness.

"Brain freeze?"

A quick swallow to clear my mouth made that true. "Yeah."

Without glancing down, he palmed the other cup and drank slowly. "I'm starting to like this flavor."

Certain he hadn't spiked my drink with a truth spell or a worse additive, I settled in for the ride.

Not long after, he pulled onto a winding dirt road with nothing but trees for miles.

"What caused this dryad to go off the rails?" I sat up to pay attention. "They're usually pretty chill."

"The paperwork says pollution in the water supply where she sprouted caused a psychotic break, but it's rare for a dryad to land on our radar. As you said, they're pretty chill. They don't cause problems."

"Do you have the file on you?"

For a beat, Asa drummed his fingers on the wheel. "It's on the floorboard behind my seat."

Clay, who couldn't fit shotgun easily, must have left it back there when he finished reading.

"This says *magical* pollution." I skimmed for more details. "It doesn't say what kind. That's important, right?"

"No one expected this to escalate. Another case of allowing preconceived notions to color expectation."

The bulk of the vehicle made parking fun, assuming we wanted to get out again without requiring a tow.

The SUV Clay had arrived in was nowhere in sight, which puzzled me, but there were other roads.

"Are you armed?" Asa reached into the console to retrieve his service weapon. "Or do you need to be?"

The modified Glock used ensorcelled rounds that blasted magical shrapnel throughout a target's body.

"I'm good." I patted the leather pouch. "I brought my own firepower."

Interest sparked in his eyes before he slid out his door onto the grass. Interest in my magic. Not in me.

After giving his drink the stink eye, I joined him in the field and did a thing I rarely did these days.

I drew my wand.

The length of twisted wood resembled a crooked finger and had come from the magnolia tree that grew above my mother's grave. Most wands required an emotional link to infuse the carved base with power.

For white witches, it was a familial element. For black witches, it was a link to an important death.

For me, it was both those things. I hadn't traded wands when I changed disciplines. Mine covered both.

A steady thumping noise drew us deeper into the woods, where all suspicion Asa had ulterior motives in bringing me along vanished as we discovered the spot where the agent in charge of this retrieval lost her life.

Death didn't bother me. I had caused too much of it to be squeamish. But this was a bad way to go.

The killing blow crushed the woman's skull. The dryad had decided to smash her brain to jelly for funsies.

I squatted next to the body, as if there could be any doubt the woman was dead, and there it was...

A tingle along my senses that alerted me to the presence of power ripe for harvesting.

Her heart was intact, and like an addict jonesing for a hit, I salivated as I stared at her chest.

"Clay must be over there."

On a breath that was part mercy and part desperation, I murmured a spell and touched the wand to her.

The body incinerated in a fever-bright rush of magic pulled straight from my core, leaving fine white dust that would scatter on the winds, lifting her soul to whatever afterlife she believed in.

And, most importantly, destroying her heart before I cheated on my diet.

A warm hand rested on my shoulder, and that touch made it easier to shake off my mood and rise.

"Thank you for that." Asa made a gesture at his navel that reminded me of a Catholic signing the cross.

"We all deserve last rites." Pitiful as they might be. "Let's find Clay."

Golem or not, Clay had his breaking point. We had to reach him before a rabbi was required for repairs.

A steady *thump, thump, thump* guided us straight to him, and the dryad.

The nature spirit had inhabited a rotting pecan tree, but that didn't limit her reach. The roots had ripped from the earth, leaving them to slither across the dirt in search of anchors for when it swatted at a foe it was having trouble pulping.

Clay might not be fast, but he moved well, and he was tough.

"Need help?" I kept a safe distance from the tree. "Or is this a con job to get us to do the work for you?"

A turn of his head revealed the far side of his face. "Shish look like a con shob to you?"

Had he been anything other than golem, he would have been dead. The first blow might not have done it, but it would have put him on the ground, and that was the last place you wanted to be during a fight.

An inch to the left, and she would have destroyed his *shem*, leaving her with a clay statue to pummel.

From the corner of my eye, I spotted a black SUV up a tree and wondered if she smacked him with it.

"I can take her down," Asa said from beside me, "but it won't be pretty."

"I haven't done the white witch thing in the field," I confessed with a twinge of embarrassment, because honesty with your partner, even a temporary one, kept you both alive that much longer. "I might need a helping hand once I expel the dryad from the tree."

"I'm right here." Hearing Asa say so shouldn't have made a difference, but it did.

I didn't trust Asa. To be fair, I didn't know him. But I trusted how Clay behaved toward him.

A direct order could force him to vouch for Asa with me, but it couldn't make him like the guy.

Clay didn't give nicknames to people he didn't like. Well, okay, nicknames used in the person's presence.

"Here goes nothing," I muttered under my breath. "Wand, don't fail me now."

A black witch had power in proportion to the amount of magic she consumed, aka hearts eaten.

A white witch had spells, charms, or potions from her spell kit, made in advance, and her own essence.

If I swaggered into the ring bent on reliving my glory days, more like *gory* days, I would KO myself.

Prowling closer to the enraged pecan tree, I let Clay do the hard work of distracting the dryad while I got in position behind her. The downside of using a wand was the fact it required contact with its target. The flick-your-wrist spell-slinging in movies was wishful thinking. Wands were conduits for power and intent. I had to mentally prep a spell and then make a conscious choice to unleash it on someone or something.

The wand was thirteen inches long, which meant I had to get close. Handy as a cloaking spell would have been right about now, I couldn't risk expending my power willy-nilly until I rediscovered my limits.

I was out of practice sneaking, but I crept in until three feet separated me from the splintering trunk.

"Black witch," the dryad spat. "I smell the death caked on your soul."

A limb wider than my waist swept in an arc that almost knocked my head off my shoulders.

"You're no better than I am." I dove into a roll. "I saw your handiwork a few minutes ago."

"You're wrong." Blistering rage shook her leaves. "I'm not like you."

A hard yank on my ankle dumped me on the ground. A rootlet was hauling me within killing range.

Gathering my will, I pushed power from my core into the wand then struck the hairy root with its tip.

Smoke sizzled down its length, gaining speed as it ran up the trunk like reverse lightning, cooking the old limbs and charring the dead leaves.

A scream rang out as a pale blur was expelled from the tree. The creature sat up, blinked her wide green eyes, then hooked her fingers into claws and charged me. The dress she wore glittered hot with embers.

Blinking away gold spots in my vision, I readied my wand, prepped a spell, and hoped it wouldn't kill me.

"Oh, shit."

That was Clay. Definitely Clay. But I couldn't see him.

Probably because my body gave up and fell sideways like a sack of potatoes.

One more spell was all I needed, but nope. I was out of juice and out of luck.

A bestial roar vibrated through the ground under my cheek, but whatever made it could take a number.

The line to eviscerate me was forming behind the rabid dryad.

A creature taller than Clay, from this perspective, stepped over me to stand between me and the dryad.

I don't know what compelled me to inch a hand forward until I could brush a fingertip down the back of its nearest ankle. A head injury, maybe. The skin was dark red, feverish to the touch, but black rosettes made stunning patterns over its heel. The creature tensed under my touch, torquing its muscular upper body to inspect what I was doing and whether or not I meant it harm.

The bones of its face had shifted when he did, widening his cheeks and forehead, but it was Asa.

Thick black horns curled from his temples back over his head, and his hair had come undone. There were miles of it. Black silk. I would have reached for that too if I had the strength, but I couldn't get my fingers to twitch, let alone my arm to rise.

He was still staring down at me with those burnt-crimson eyes when the dryad smacked into him. A low growl of annoyance curled his lip, revealing thick fangs, and he returned his focus to subduing her. There wasn't any doubt in my mind the dryad was beyond saving. Even if she were salvageable, the director would put her down for the death of a Black Hat agent.

Knowing both those things, I gasped when Asa punched his fist into her chest and ripped out her heart.

And I recoiled when he offered it to me on his wide palm like a gift...or a snack.

"Eat," he rumbled, blood dripping through his fingers. "Heal."

"Ace," Clay warned, his speech much improved, "that's not how she rolls anymore."

"Eat," Asa insisted. *"Heal."*

"No," I whispered as my eyelids lowered. "No."

I had come too far to fall back on old habits now.

5

A hard bump jostled me awake, and I murmured, "No jumping
on the bed."

For a moth, Colby had surprising heft. She probably
weighed a good ten pounds.

"Rue?" A warm hand cradled my cheek. "How do you feel?"

The touch flung my eyes wide open, and I got a prime view of a
half-naked Asa. "Where's your shirt?"

Oh, yeah. I was blaming brain damage for the fact his cut torso
was mesmerizing me.

"I lost it when I shifted." A furrow tightened his brow. "Do you
remember what happened?"

"The end is a little fuzzy." I moved my arm and bumped his knee.
"Am I...in your lap?"

A snort from up front confirmed it. We were back in the SUV. The
bump must have been a pothole.

"Yes," Asa said softly. "You were unconscious."

Another memory burst to the forefront of my mind, and I
clamped a hand over my mouth. "No."

I swallowed once, twice to test for any coppery aftertaste, but all

I found was dirt and a piece of grass.

"You didn't eat the heart," Asa confirmed. "You said no, and I didn't force it on you."

"Thank you." I placed my hand on my stomach. "I don't want to be that person again."

Had I caved today, I couldn't have faced Colby. I would have failed her, and myself.

A tickle on the arm tucked against Asa left me brushing long black strands off my elbow.

Caving to my earlier impulse, I smoothed the strands between my fingers. "Your hair is soft."

The SUV swerved as Clay jerked his gaze to the rearview mirror. "Rue..."

"I don't mind." Asa watched me. "You can touch it."

A laugh bubbled up the back of my throat. "That sounds so wrong."

"I agree," Clay grumbled. "You're better off keeping your hands to yourself."

A low growl vibrated through Asa as their gazes clashed in the reflection, but I was too tired to care.

"I'm going to nap now," I announced to avoid them freaking out when my eyes didn't open again.

I fell asleep with a lock of Asa's hair curled around my finger.

"Rue." The weight of a chonky house cat landed on my chest. For real this time. "Wake up."

"*Oomph.*"

"I don't weigh that much." Colby jabbed my cheek with a foot. "Open your eyes."

The nap had done me good. I wasn't back to my usual self, but I was getting there. No hearts required.

"There." I widened my eyes until they bulged as I stared down at her. "Are you happy now?"

"That's creepy." She smacked me between the eyes. "Stop being weird."

A yawn stretched my jaw, and I lifted my arms overhead, arching my back on the seat.

Oh.

Not the seat.

Heat prickled in my cheeks when I glanced up at Asa. "Um."

He cocked an eyebrow. "Yes?"

"Thank you for the use of your lap." I clutched Colby to my chest as I sat upright. "Home already?"

"I gave you thirty minutes." Colby tucked her wings in tight. "You didn't wake up, so I came out."

Magically induced exhaustion had done a number on my brain. I hadn't put together how she was here.

"You know the rules." I lifted her to my face level. "Never leave the wards."

Puffing her fur, she crossed four arms over her chest. "Clay and Asa..."

"You don't know Clay or Asa." I put us nose to proboscis. "You can't trust people you just met."

The stubborn moth had chosen her hill. "*You* trust them."

Aware both agents were watching me, one more intently than the other, I sighed. "Promise me."

"I promise," she said dutifully. "I will stay inside the wards where it's boring and nothing ever happens."

Her sass was nothing new, but I could guess why the rules chafed now when they never had before.

"Good." I kissed the top of her head. "That's what I like to hear."

Heaving a dramatic sigh, she wriggled free and glided to the house in the next best thing to slow motion.

"That kid." I wiped my mouth to check for drool. "I'm not sure this is wise."

"The paperwork came through while you were resting." Asa cut the legs out from under my argument. "The director is willing to work with you on a case-by-case basis. He's willing to permit you to live here, if you touch base with your team once a week during times when you're not on an active case."

For him to agree to such big concessions, he wanted me back for more than this copycat case.

That might change once he heard about my new dietary restrictions.

But I doubted it.

Something else Asa said struck a belated chord with me. "My team?"

"You have to be on call twenty-four-seven to rate a partner." Clay chuckled. "Part-timers get a team."

I could see where this was headed from a mile away, but I still asked, "Do I get to pick them?"

A preternatural stillness swept over Asa. "Yes."

"Hmm." I tapped a finger against my bottom lip. "Can I interview candidates or...?"

"Yes." Asa angled his face away from me. "That can be arranged."

"She's pulling your leg, Ace." Clay snorted. "She wants us."

"You got your butt kicked by a tree earlier." I could laugh about it now. "I'm not sure you're qualified."

"That's not fair." The car rocked when he twisted to face us. "I had already pulverized seven trees by the time you got there." He cut me a scowl that highlighted his pulpy face. "Plus, I've got Ace up my sleeve."

I shouldn't have laughed, but I couldn't help myself. He looked ready to climb in the back and shake me. Between the grinding and popping noises the seat was making, I doubted it would hold out much longer.

"Clay, you know you're the only one I trust to hold my umbrella at the shitshow."

A wide grin swept across his face, and he pumped his fist, leaving a dent in the roof.

With Asa's head turned, it was hard to gauge, but I detected a lip twitch at Clay's enthusiasm.

A single tap on Asa's hand where it rested on the seat earned me his full attention.

"You had my back." I searched his face. "I won't forget that." I stuck out my hand. "Teammates?"

His warm fingers wrapped mine and didn't let go. "Teammates."

"Details are in your inbox." Clay grunted when he caught his hip under the steering wheel. "Let us—"

Snap. Crack. Pop.

A yelp shot out of me when the seat broke, dropping it—and Clay —into my lap.

"Hold still." Asa set his hand on Clay's shoulder. "You're going to crush her legs."

The golem twisted his lips, but that was all he moved. "Sorry, Dollface."

"Accidents happen." I was just glad Colby had gone in. "There's a reason you're a backseat driver."

"I'll have to shift to get it off you." Asa lifted his eyebrows. "It'll be a tight fit."

"Do what you gotta do." I wiggled my toes. "I'm losing feeling below the knee."

Flame exploded down the length of Asa's frame, igniting a change that resulted in the same beast from the forest sitting next to me. Mostly. He had to duck to make allowances for his horns, and his upper body required him to crowd me.

The daemon braced one wide palm on the seat behind me then cupped the broken front seat, shoving it upright and holding it steady while Clay contorted enough to ease out the driver side door.

"I'm clear." He reached in and took the weight of the seat from the daemon, holding it off me. "Scoot out."

"Stay," the daemon ordered me then performed a contortionist act of his own to get out his door.

"I could just..." I hooked my thumb toward my open door. "I'm bruised, but nothing's broken."

The daemon didn't appear to trust my self-diagnosis. He wedged a hand under my thighs, placed one on my back, and lifted me out of the SUV and against his bare chest. Now that he had me, he appeared torn on what to do with me. Wards prevented him from entering the yard or house, and the SUV was busted.

"You can set me down here." I pointed to a patch of thick grass. "I promise not to budge."

The daemon snorted, not believing me for a hot minute, but the movement brought his hair gliding over his wide shoulder into my lap. His burnt-crimson eyes watched me for a moment, daring me to play with it as I had in the SUV earlier.

Maybe it was an inkling that Asa viewed himself as monstrous that made me slide my fingers through the silken length while he purred around me.

"You really don't want to do that," Clay warned me. "Ace, put her down and shift."

Wide fangs sharpened the corners of his smile. "No."

As much as I hated playing the damsel, I had witnessed this type of overprotective behavior triggered in predatory males when their female partners got hurt before. Wargs were terrible about it. Gwyllgi weren't any better. Big cat shifters might be the worst. Even vampires got extra bitey over opposite-sex partners.

Daemons must have the same instinctive drive to care for us puny females under their protection.

"I'm going to let go of your hair." I opened my hand. "And now you're going to let go of me."

The daemon's brows slammed down, and he looked like he was thinking about growling at me.

Done humoring him, I murmured a tiny spell and jabbed him with my finger. I only had enough juice for a static shock, which was laughable on a daemon his size. But it did the job. He lost his focus. That gave me an opening to shove off his chest, flip over his arms, and land in a crouch.

"Ace." Clay snapped his fingers in his partner's face. "I will kick your ass if you take another step."

A tinkling laugh froze us all in place, and we turned in unison to the porch and the moth on the railing.

"You say a *lot* of bad words." Colby fluttered with delight. "More than my gamer friends even."

As I straightened, I leveled a stare on her. "Your gamer friends use language around you?"

"I hear the microwave beeping." She spun in a circle. "Gotta go."

"Can she use the microwave?"

"Oh, yes." I found Clay standing beside me, half his attention on the daemon. "She enjoys explosions."

Moths weren't meant to microwave, but that didn't stop her from trying to cook when I wasn't home. I was shocked she hadn't burned down the house as often as she zapped tinfoil. And utensils. And metal takeout containers.

For a while, I thought it was a cry for attention. Then I realized, no. She was just that bad in the kitchen. Since she was always trying to fix me dinner or desserts for special occasions when disaster struck, I didn't fuss.

Alarm clanged through his tone. "How...?"

"She watches a lot of TikTok." She got me hooked too. "It gives her ideas."

The thirst traps I fell into on total and complete accident gave me ideas too.

"I should go." I backed away to keep the daemon in sight. "I need to read over that contract."

No doubt there was fine print buried in there ready to trip me up if I didn't comb over it.

"You do that." Clay waved to the moth with her proboscis glued to the drama. "See you tomorrow."

This twenty-four-hour window Asa sold me on was stretching into a solid forty-eight.

"I have to make the right decision." I had to say it, even as it caused Clay to drop his smile. "For her."

"Team," the daemon growled, "mates."

I heard the gap between those words, and it gave me a case of the shivers. The daemon in Asa had ideas about me. I chose to believe Asa was reading into the bond I shared with Clay, and the day's events gave him a case of overprotectivitis. That I could forgive. You couldn't change your DNA.

And just like that, I dumped a bucket of ice-cold reality over my own head.

Sure, I resisted temptation today. That didn't mean it wouldn't consume me tomorrow.

Each case was another opportunity to succumb, another heart no one would mind me having for lunch.

"Once you sign on the dotted line, I'll get the files to you." Clay kept a wary eye on the daemon. "Well, he will."

The size of Clay's fingers made it hard for him to use laptops. Phones, at least, could be voice controlled.

Inching back, I banged the fence with my hip, fumbled the gate open behind me, then retreated into the yard, safe behind the wards. All without turning my back on the daemon, who watched me with avarice.

Manners I had forgotten returned to me in a rush now that a ward stood between me and the daemon.

Already dreading the answer, I still forced out, "Do you need a lift to your hotel?"

"Yes," the daemon rumbled, his fangs gleaming.

"No." Clay spoke over him. "I called a tow for the SUV. The driver said he would give us a lift into town."

"Sounds like you boys have it handled." I pivoted on my heel. "I'll be inside if you need anything."

A shiver coasted down my spine, and I glanced over my shoulder to find the daemon sliding a dark claw down the ward that kept him from opening the gate.

6

After Colby fell asleep in her faux-forest bedroom, I retreated into mine to scry for legal help.

Cross-legged on the bed, I sat with a mixing bowl cradled between my thighs. A drop of blood got the party started, and I dialed, for lack of a better word, an old friend from beyond the veil. With Halloween around the corner, the connection ought to be crystal clear.

"Megara, I summon thee." More blood, more intent. "Megara, I summon thee."

The stubborn wench refused to show until I jumped through all the hoops, which probably explained why she was aces with contracts.

"Thrice I bid thee." Even more blood, even more intent. "And thrice I tithe thee."

I ran a fingertip along the edge of the bowl, and the water rippled, darkened, swirled in a mini whirlpool.

"Hear me," I called in a resonate voice. "Arise."

A face appeared wreathed in smoke, not from theatrics, but from the cigarette hanging from her bottom lip. I had baked bread pudding with raisins that had fewer wrinkles than Meg, but I wouldn't accept legal advice from a dessert, no matter how delicious it might be. Meg, on the other hand, had practiced law in one form or another for a good three hundred years before she took a silver bullet to the heart.

"Your form is rusty, darling," she chided in a deep rasp. "How long has it been?"

"Eight years." I squirmed under her disapproval. "Time flies when you're having fun."

"Fun?" Her eyes, hidden beneath folds of papery skin, narrowed on me. "You're having fun?"

"Not particularly?"

"Oh, but you are." She sat back. "Your cheeks are flush, your eyes are bright, and your heart is racing."

"You can't tell that last part."

"Let's call it an educated guess." She glanced at the bed behind me. "Where is he?"

"Who?"

"The man who put that glow about you."

"There is no man." I hesitated. "Actually, there is a man. Sort of."

"Mmm-hmm." Her lips spread, lipstick spiking the creases. "Tell me all about him."

"It's Clay."

"Darling, no." She shook her cigarette at me. "He's a good boy, don't get me wrong, but he's..."

"Not anatomically correct?"

"Precisely."

I could have educated her on how that didn't slow him down from pursuing his interests, but I was afraid tiny ears might overhear. I did *not* want to explain the battery-operated birds and the bees to a moth.

"Black Hat found me." I redirected her. "They want me back."

"They never let you go," she said sadly. "Albert would rather die than part with you."

The director's name wasn't spoken, to avoid drawing his attention, but the veil was beyond even his reach.

"I negotiated the terms of my return with the agents they sent after me. I have a contract."

"I will have to charge my standard fee, you understand, but I can look over it now if you like."

"That's more than fair."

The transfer of one thousand dollars to her former pack's alpha went through in seconds, and I held the screen up as proof. That she chose to help the loved ones she left behind made me happy to contribute.

"Okay." She settled in on her side of the divide. "Get your pen and paper ready then start reading."

The biggest downside with using a deceased lawyer was the time commitment.

Meg couldn't very well reach through the ether and accept a printed copy, so I had to read and notate. I got a discount for having to play paralegal for her, for which I was grateful, but it meant I wouldn't sleep much tonight. Not that sleep and I were on a first-name basis these days. Or ever, really.

There was a soothing rhythm to the collaborative process, but that came from years of working together anytime I got twitchy about papers I was asked to sign.

I hadn't met Meg while she was alive, though she had been friends with my mother. We met when she executed my parents' wills from the beyond, and it hurt too much to surrender that link when I would never see them again.

Black witches have no afterlife. We simply stop. Here one day, gone forever the next.

I had been taught that we consumed so much life on this side of the veil we ate through our afterlives.

I wasn't sure what I believed. If I believed anything at all. It hadn't bothered me, none of it, until Colby.

Not even when Mom, a powerful white witch, failed to appear no matter how often I scried for her.

Six hours later, I squinted at words as they swam across the page, ready to sign anything to get sleep.

"That ought to do it." Megara took a puff. "Let me know if you need more assistance."

"I will." I yawned. "Thanks."

"I wasn't wrong about your glow." She blew smoke against her side of the barrier. "I mistook its origin."

The safest response I could manage was, "Oh?"

"The thrill of the hunt." Her eyes gleamed with approval. "Your predatory nature is awakening."

"That's the last thing I want." I studied the notes spread around me. "I don't want to regress."

"Your mother ran with our pack on the full moon." She laughed at the memory. "Naked as a jaybird."

That woke me up with a cringe. "What did Dad think of that?"

"This was before your father tamed some of her wildness." She curled her lip. "The point is, you are your mother's daughter. You'll always have her fierce spirit. Your father was a good man." She rolled a hand. "As far as black witches go." She shook her head. "I can't blame him for falling in love with her. What she saw in him? That, I'll never know, but God as my witness, she loved him more than anything. Until you."

"I have to walk a path that doesn't haunt me for the rest of my life."

Curling smoke cast shadows onto her features. "I know, darling."

"This contract is as good as it gets for people like me."

"It's a breadcrumb." Her mouth pinched. "Follow that path, and you know where it leads."

Right back to the loaf. Or maybe the bakery? One or the other.

"Clay says they've got a Silver Stag copycat. He—or she—is taking young girls in groups of four."

"Albert couldn't have baited his hook better if he cut them to chum the waters himself."

That painted a vivid mental picture I wouldn't soon forget. "Do you think he's involved?"

"No," she sighed her disappointment. "Black Hat's reputation for training monsters to hunt their own is his legacy. He would never tarnish the Bureau's reputation and would kill to keep its record spotless."

"I'm going to finish this counteroffer then crash." I rubbed itchy eyes. "Thanks for your help."

"Next time, dial me up for a chat." She flicked ash off her cigarette. "It doesn't have to be all business."

"I will," I promised, and I meant it. "Night, Megara."

"Good night, darling."

Careful not to spill water on my bed, I carried the mixing bowl to the bathroom to pour down the drain.

Leave a metaphysical doorway open and who knew what might drift through it. The same rules applied to scrying. People who wielded black magic didn't live long if they got sloppy with it.

With the bowl drained, washed, and set on the sink to dry, I climbed back in bed to organize my notes.

An hour later, I was happy to scan the pages with my phone and email them to Asa to hand up the chain.

So close to dawn, I didn't expect an immediate response from him, but I got one.

A text.

>>*I apologize for my behavior.*

As much as I would love to claim I fired off a quip about how he always seemed to be apologizing to me, I debated how to answer until I fell asleep.

Morning came seconds after my head hit the pillow. That was how it felt, anyway. I strangled my phone, which was bleating its usual *time for work* alarm, until it shut up and left me alone.

"Hey."

The tiny whisper almost brought tears to my eyes. I did not want to get out of bed yet.

"Hey, Rue."

Maybe if I ignored it, it would go away.

"The daemon from last night is on our porch."

That did it.

My eyes flew open, my heart lodged in my throat, and my feet swung over the edge of the bed.

"Wards?" I wiped my mouth with the back of my hand. "Breach?"

Soft feet tickled up my leg until a guilty-looking moth sat on my lap. "I lied about the daemon."

The starch went out of me, and I fell back, but the adrenaline churning in my veins refused to quit.

"He's not on the porch," she continued, climbing up my stomach to sit on my chest. "He's in the yard."

"Why?" I wasn't sure if I was asking her about Asa, or the universe about why I was awake, or why she was attempting to give me a heart attack.

"He was there when I woke up this morning. Not daemon-Asa. Just regular Asa." She stared down at me. "And before you fuss, I've been calling your name *forever*, and I really need to get back to my game."

The downside of my brand of insomnia was when I finally did fall sleep, I was dead to the world. That explained why I didn't rouse when she called my name. It had nothing to do with my subconscious perking up at learning Asa was right outside.

None of which sounded great for my peace of mind. "Clay?"

"I haven't seen him."

Eyes sliding closed, I mumbled, "I'll handle it."

Colby pounced on my gut, knocking the wind out of me, then zipped out the door in a blur.

"That was cruel," I wheezed after her, "and horrible and plain mean."

"I had to make sure you didn't roll over and go back to sleep."

"For that, no high-speed internet for a month. It's dial-up for you."

Popping her head around the doorframe, she quivered her antennae. "What's dial-up?"

"Leave." I flicked my hand at her. "Your youth disgusts me."

A quick check confirmed that nope, I hadn't taken off yesterday's clothes.

Grit in my eyes and tangles in my hair, I padded through the house until I stood on the front porch.

Asa leaned against a tree, whittling a stick he no doubt found in my yard.

For no good reason, that irked me. "Can I help you?"

He wore his standard Bureau-issued suit that made me hot looking at him.

Not like hot-hot, I meant sweaty. Not like good-sex sweaty, just regular sweaty.

And gods above, could I see him once and not have dirty thoughts?

"I came for your signature." He straightened from his lean. "We got a phone call."

That first day, Clay told me the copycat killer phoned in his crimes after he committed them.

A heavy weight pressed on my chest, a question of whether I could have made a difference to these girls if I had been less invested in protecting Colby, and myself. But one thing life had taught me was that you had to take care of you. No one else would do it for you.

This was not my fault. These deaths were not on my head.

But the next time, and there would be a next time and a next until we stopped him, it might be.

If I didn't sign away my soul, I might cost someone else theirs.

Four someones.

There was only one response I could live with, assuming the amendments held. "Do you have a pen?"

"Yes." He exchanged his knife for a pen and stuck his carving in the dirt. "I'll get the papers."

A faded blanket was spread across the ground behind him, its earth tones too muted for me to notice at first.

The file holding the contract rested in the center, along with a thermos I bet was filled with black coffee.

It was on the tip of my tongue to ask if he had spent the night out here, but he was too fresh for that. He had returned his hair to its usual long braids and traded his oval earrings for dainty silver hoops to match the one in his nose. *Dainty* wasn't the right word, but I was staring again, and I couldn't get my brain or vocabulary to function.

"Where's Clay?" I scanned the driveway, but there was no sign of him. "How did you get here?"

Last night, I waited until after the tow truck left with its passengers before summoning Megara.

Between then and now, Clay would have secured them transportation. Either a rental or a company SUV could have been delivered, even this far out in the sticks.

"I went hunting last night." He retrieved the folder. "I shouldn't have left it so long. It caused me to..."

"...get territorial?"

"Yes." He held out the papers with the pen on top. "I apologize for my behavior."

Last night came back to me in a rush, and I let myself out of the gate. "Your text."

"It was cowardly of me not to apologize in person."

The reason I got rolled out of bed came back too. "Is that why you felt the need to stake out my yard?"

"Yes," he said with enough hesitation I doubted it was his only reason.

"I got your text, but I was up late working on the contract. I fell asleep before I could respond."

The contract was the exact version Megara and I drafted, and it was already signed by the director at the bottom.

"I'll run in and sign this at the table." I nudged open the gate. "Can I get you anything?"

"No." He crouched, retrieved his stick, and resumed his whittling. "Thank you."

No surprise, Colby met me at the door and trailed me to the kitchen table.

Palms spreading over the stack, I murmured a soft chant that would verify my assumption.

"The contract is identical." Not so much as a punctuation mark had been corrected. "That's good."

"Then why are you scowling at it?" Colby sat on the papers. "You don't have to do this, you know."

For me.

She left that part unspoken.

"Life is about compromise." I scratched her head. "I do this, and we get to keep our life here."

"We could run again." She patted my hand with a foot. "We could buy another house, right?"

"I've spent a stupid amount of money Colby-sizing your game room. I'm not leaving it behind."

That was only part of the truth, and she knew it, but she didn't want to make this about her.

How much she recalled of her ordeal, I couldn't say, and she wouldn't tell me. She preferred to pretend I found her wild and tamed her. It hurt less than remembering she had been a little girl once, with parents and a family and a dog.

I collected pictures of them off social media and printed them to hang on her walls when she first came to live with me, but I found them balled up in the garbage. I tried again each time we moved, but I was starting to believe my need to fix unfixable things where she was concerned was more for me than her.

"I heard Megara." She rolled the pen back and forth. "You do seem happier."

"I missed Clay." I couldn't say his name without smiling. "I didn't realize how much."

"It's hard hiding who and what you are from your friends." Her antennae swiveled. "It's like, okay, they're your friends, but would they still be your friends if they knew the *real* you?"

This wasn't about me, not really, but that was the safest way to address the answer.

"Sometimes the face you show one person might not be what another one sees. Our friends share our interests, but not *all* our interests. It's okay to have different ones for different things. That a person only knows one side of you doesn't make them any less your friend."

"No one here knows you're a witch," she said thoughtfully, "so Clay is your witch-stuff friend."

"Exactly." I let her mull over that. "The relationship I have with him isn't like the one I have with Arden and Camber. They have different hobbies than he does." I poked her side. "Like viral food videos and cute boys."

Antennae quivering, she stared up at me with big, round eyes. "What's our thing?"

"*Every*thing." I kissed the top her head. "It's hard hiding secrets from your roomie."

Happiness twitching in her wings, she scooted off the contract. "You going to sign or what?"

After I signed my life away, I sat back, half expecting my soul to be contractually ripped from my body.

Nothing happened.

Either because I was overly dramatic or had no soul or maybe both.

The stack of papers shimmered under my hand. It was the only warning I got before they disappeared.

"Whoa." Colby walked a circle where they had been. "Where did they go?"

A sour taste hit the back of my throat. "Straight to the director's desk."

Much like the mythical Satan, he was the final word on all binding contracts.

"That's so cool." A shiver worked through her. "You're a witch and all, but you never do witchy stuff."

"You're just mad because I refused to enchant the kitchen to bake for you on command."

Rainbows and kittens might as well have burst from her eyes as she rounded them for full effect.

"I would blow things up less if you did..."

"Are you trying to tell me you blow things up on purpose, so I'll cave to your demands?"

A heartbeat passed as I watched the calculations run behind her eyes. "Gotta go."

Quick as a flash, she kicked off the table and zoomed back into her game room.

"Spoiled brat," I grumbled loud enough for her to hear. "No respect for your elders."

The weight of the pen in my hand brought my attention back to who waited for me.

I had done the deed. Signed my name. Accepted my fate. And maybe, I would do some good.

I was a willing employee, as willing as any Black Hat, and it was time to pay the piper.

"I'm going to talk to Asa," I called, figuring she was already plugged in. "Stay inside the wards."

He met me at the gate, and it was silly to be more comfortable with the ward between us when I just did the unthinkable by returning to Black Hat, which entailed a formal agreement to work with Clay and Asa.

"It's done." I worried one of the claw marks I would have to repair later. "I'm official."

The peridot of his eyes was eclipsed by burnt crimson for a split second. "I'll send the case files then."

"Clay's still not here?" I checked the road, but I could see it was clear for miles. "Where is he?"

"At the hotel." He examined the claw marks too, or maybe the tips of my fingers. "I put him in stasis last night while the enchantment repaired the damage from the dryad."

"He hates that." I couldn't blame him. "How much longer does he have?"

For Clay, he could still hear and see what happened around him. He was paralyzed, not sleeping.

"I'm going to head back now." He backed up a step. "You have my number if you have any questions."

"You're going to walk back?" The sun was up now, and so were my neighbors. "The whole way?"

"Yes?" He canted his head. "I walked out here. Ran, actually."

Groggy from my wakeup, I missed the big picture earlier. "You hunted in *my* backyard?"

"Your yard is warded." He smiled the tiniest bit. "I hunted in your neighbor's yard."

"This isn't going to be a problem, is it?" I gestured between us. "Whatever *this* is."

Without answering me, he turned on his heel to go, with that pleased-as-pie look on his face.

He made it to the end of my driveway before I caved to my better nature.

"Wait," I called to him. "I'll drive you."

Rushing inside, I changed clothes and pulled up my hair. "Colby, I'm heading to work."

No answer.

No surprise there.

I scribbled a note that said the same and stuck it to the pantry where I kept her pollen.

Asa waited for me with one hand in his pocket. When I rolled to a stop beside him, he made no move to get in. I stared at him. He stared right back. I considered driving over his foot. He only widened his smile.

Giving in to him, a dangerous habit to start, I leaned across the seat and shoved open his door.

"You are one weird dude." I strapped on my seat belt. "Why did you stand there?"

"You had to invite me in."

A laugh burst out of me. "Are you serious?"

"No." He laughed too, softer. "I was teasing."

After the drama from yesterday, he was trying to make amends. I appreciated that, and I decided I might not want to beat him to death with his own shoe after all. Daemon culture wasn't a subject I had studied with my parents or later, with Black Hat, though some witches specialized in summoning the nastier ones.

From my general studies, I couldn't peg Asa's caste. He didn't behave like any daemon mentioned in the darker texts that had been my focus. Maybe his fae blood was to blame. I wasn't sure, and it was rude to ask. Worse, it would open me up to questions like *So, were you born evil, or did you choose to be?*

For a black witch, there was only one answer. For me? I wasn't so sure anymore.

The radio kept us entertained on the way to town, and I dropped Asa off at his hotel to free Clay.

As much as I hated to abandon my store, I didn't have much choice. I couldn't balance both jobs without dropping one or the other, and the case had to be my priority. I had my speech planned out when Arden glanced up from the counter and pointed to voices coming from the back room.

I followed the conversation to Miss Dotha, who sat behind my desk. Hunched over my desktop, Camber beside her, she had started on filling online orders that needed to go out on our next mail drop. Her glasses had slid to the end of her nose, which almost touched the screen, but her cheeks were flush with purpose.

Miss Dotha, being farsighted, had no trouble spotting me across the room. "What are you doing here?"

"I work here?"

Camber snorted then straightened when Miss Dotha gave her side-eye. "Why aren't you on vacation?"

While the girls believed I was helping the police put my abusive ex behind bars, Miss Dotha, and the rest of the town, got the much more vanilla excuse of me taking a trip to the mountains.

"I came to break the news to the girls." I smoothed an eyebrow. "I see you have things under control."

"Gran told me you called her to set things up," Camber confessed, "and I told Arden."

The phone tree was a real thing in this town. Probably everyone and their momma knew I was leaving.

"Was there something else?" Miss Dotha resumed her hunch. "I'm on the clock here."

"No, ma'am." I meekly backed out of the office—*my* office—and bumped into the counter. "Have fun."

"She's not so bad." Arden straightened the flyers I knocked askew. "But also, please, come back soon."

Laughing at her darted glances toward the back room, I left her to fend for herself. Miss Dotha might as well be a blood relative, as much time as the girls spent together. Arden loved her, even if Miss Dotha could be prickly.

The store hadn't taken any time at all, so I popped into the smoothie shop to get my breakfast of choice. I hesitated but then decided to get Asa the same thing. I chose the daily specials for Clay, who would eat or drink anything you set in front of him. One of each. Both large.

When my order came up, I scratched an *R* in the foam near the bottom of my cup with a thumbnail. I felt ten kinds of stupid but also eaten up with curiosity. I had to know if I was off my rocker, and this was an eight-dollar sanity check. Not that it explained why he may or may not be playing switcheroo with me.

Armed with breakfast, I returned to the hotel for a debriefing and to dig into the files in person.

Negotiations had cost us time, but I couldn't regret the precautions I had taken for Colby and me.

Clay met me at the door with a scowl I recognized as him shaking off the sedative effect of self-repair.

"Maybe this will help." I passed him the first of his drinks. "Blueberry banana with granola."

"Thanks." He gestured me into their suite. "Don't mind if I do."

Asa sat at the table that was the reason for the suite, in my experience, with papers strewn about him.

"I got you my usual." I presented him with the cup. "You seemed to like it well enough yesterday."

"Thank you." He accepted the offering then kicked the leg of the chair across from him to push it out for me. "I didn't expect you to finish your errands so soon."

"The problem with hiring good people and training them well is they don't need you." I placed my cup five or six inches from his, on my side of the table, then did my level best to ignore it. "I have a few things for Colby to do, but nothing major. I can be ready to leave from home within an hour."

"You're leaving Colby?" Clay traded out for his second drink. "Will she be okay with that?"

The alternative, parading her around in front of my fellow Black Hats, wasn't happening.

Humans might mistake her for a hair bow, but other paranormals would sense her magic and salivate.

"Colby is safer at home than she would be with me on the road."

Before we moved in, I warded the house like a fortress in case Black Hat caught up to us at home. Colby knew her way around our property. There were thirteen moth-sized emergency shelters, each six-inches square and protected by individual wards, in case the worst happened.

The target was on my back, which gave Colby an excellent chance of escaping while in her smallest form.

"She's your ward." Asa spread his hands. "You know best."

Until he mentioned it, I hadn't noticed how hard I was silently daring him to claim it was a bad idea. But that was my insecurities talking. I had done my best. I had planned for the worst. Now we tested it.

"I'm worried." I sipped my smoothie. "I can't put her in my pocket and carry her everywhere I go."

Life would be simpler for me, but she wouldn't really be living, and that was the whole point of all this.

Clay sat on the bed, a safer bet than the spindly chairs. "How much does she remember?"

"All of it." I took another sip to wet my parched throat. "She won't talk about it, but it's in there."

The burnt-black eyes of Asa's daemon stared out at me. "Only a true monster preys on children."

Monster had so many definitions. I didn't disagree with his, but mine must be broader.

"Talk to me about the phone calls." I accepted the bulky file from him. "You heard from the killer this morning?"

"The lead team did, yes." Clay shifted his weight on the bed, much to the unhappiness of its springs. "He dialed up Marty at eight this morning, same time as usual, and gave him the coordinates for the herd."

The herd.

A shiver tripped down my spine at the familiar nickname for the Silver Stag victims.

"That's new." I skimmed the first page. A more in-depth read would have to wait. "The Silver Stag left his victims where they fell. He lost interest after he killed them. They ceased to exist for him."

I had met cold eyes in the mirror every morning back then, but his had been arctic. Barren. Empty.

"The copycat is making a production of their deaths." I reached the first picture and fully grasped how much I had changed since leaving Black Hat. "He's arranging the bodies." I flipped to the next. "This scene is staged." And then the next. "He cares more about the death than the hunt."

"That's what our profiler says too." Asa leaned forward, elbows on the table. "What else?"

"I'm not sure this is a copycat." I smoothed a thumb over the last photo. "What made the director so sure?"

"We'll have to fly to Asheville if you want to see for yourself."

The last thing I wanted to see was another set of victims like the previous ones. Those still haunted me.

"All right." I shut the file. "Pick me up in an hour." I got to my feet. "I'll read on the plane."

Memorization was a cornerstone of teaching for witches. A dud spell often equaled a dead witch. I was a dab hand at cramming relevant information into my brain, where it lingered until my head hit the pillow.

Smoothie in hand, I exited the hotel, got in my car, and drove home.

Only when I sat in the safety of my own driveway did I check the cup for my initial.

There was no *R* to be found.

Now I had proof of shenanigans, but what did it mean? And why did it make me want to pay him back? With interest?

7

The bulk of my prep work was done as far as Colby was concerned, for which I was grateful. I kept her six months' worth of pollen in the pantry, along with enough sugar to put the whole town in a sugar coma. I wasn't a fan of her mixing sugar water herself, so I filled a bathtub with scalding water and created a huge batch in there. After sterilizing it. Magically. Colby might be a moth, but she had standards.

The go bag I kept ready would do me in a pinch, but it had become a comfort object of sorts. I decided to leave it and pack a suitcase for a week. I refused to be apart from Colby longer than that. If I had to drop in to grab fresh clothes and a hug, then go, I was fine with that.

"The wards are dialed up to the max." I checked to be sure I had everything. "There's food in the pantry. Sugar water's in the tub. There are snacks in the cabinet." I opened my arms and let her fly to me. "Be a good girl, and don't spend the next seven days with your nose pressed to the screen. Get some fresh air."

Left to her own devices, she might never take off her headset or vacate her custom chair.

"I will," she said dutifully, but I don't think either of us believed her.

After she fluttered off with an extra shake in her butt I didn't trust, I wheeled my suitcase onto the porch.

I didn't have to wait long for Clay and Asa to arrive in a different, but identical, SUV.

The rear passenger door swung open before the vehicle stopped rolling, and Clay popped out with a bounce in his step and a swing in his chin-length red hair.

"There she is," he boomed, slapping his hands together. "Good to have you back, partner." He winced. "I mean, former partner and current teammate." He eyed my bag. "Still packing light, huh? Good deal."

Less luggage gave him more room to play Tetris with his wig boxes.

"You're good to go?" He jerked his chin toward the house. "I don't want to rush you."

But he ought to, given the stakes of the game I was once again playing.

"Colby is set." I lifted my bag. "Can you open the back?"

Asa, who had been sitting behind the wheel seconds earlier, opened it for me. "I'll take it."

"Okay." I handed it over, not caring who hefted it in there. The spell kit was what mattered, and I was wearing it. "Thanks."

When I stepped back, I bumped into Clay, who locked gazes with Asa over my head. He waited until the daemon was in the SUV, with the doors shut, to frown down at me. There was nothing he could say that Asa wouldn't overhear, which meant he kept his mouth shut, but his eyes said plenty.

Granted, I didn't have the metric Clay did, but I wasn't the only one noticing Asa's peculiar behavior.

Ever the gentleman, Clay escorted me to the front passenger side and opened the door. I hopped in with a reassuring smile for him. He was such a softy and fretted worse than a mother hen for those he loved.

Pretty sure he broke speed records climbing in behind me, the angle better to keep an eye on Asa.

To keep tensions to a minimum until we found our equilibrium as a unit, I settled in to read the files. We had a long drive and a longer flight ahead of us. I wanted to be current when we hit the ground. I was in this now, fully committed, and—with Colby safe at home—I could throw myself headlong into the case.

As much as I wished Megara was wrong about how the hunt got my blood pumping, I couldn't deny part of me had missed this camaraderie with those who understood, or at least appreciated, my struggle. The life I built for Colby and me was uncomplicated, downright wholesome, and everything my battered soul had craved for so long. But this...this felt right too.

Maybe I was wrong.

Maybe black and white weren't the only options.

Maybe, just maybe, gray areas did exist for people like me.

We touched down in Asheville, claimed our new company ride, and drove to the scene of the crime.

Case details churned through my head, mixing with memories of the Silver Stag Slayings.

I had yet to see the bodies, but I already didn't like this.

"Hold on." Asa took a narrow road that led straight up, forcing our SUV to work for it. "Almost there."

The *oh crap* handle was cutting grooves into my palm by the time we leveled off, high above the trees.

Four identical black SUVs crowded a patch of raw earth exposed from a clearcutting in progress.

"We've got company." Clay whistled from the back. "Four teams." He leaned forward. "Plus us."

That was excessive, even by Black Hat standards. Yet it sent relief cascading through me. The director was in a bind if he was allocating these types of resources to a single case. That made my reclassification less a personal matter and more a professional decision. That I could handle better than the alternative.

"Marty's been lead on this, but that changes now that you're here." Clay clasped my shoulder. "We're about to relieve him of his command." He squeezed. "Just like old times."

Not half as excited as him to butt heads with former coworkers, I cringed from his enthusiasm. "He's going to love that."

Marty Talbot hated me. He used to call me the director's pet. I had been more like a caged animal.

He probably threw an office party the day I vanished and invited all his favorite haters to attend.

Asa wedged the SUV in the only open space available, and we piled out into the muck to wade in.

The woods began again less than a dozen yards from our makeshift parking lot, the trees mostly pines. It was beautiful up here, peaceful, and part of me understood why the killer had chosen it as his hunting ground.

That predatory sense was the reason why I was here, just as much as my experience with the Silver Stag.

Four or five agents had gathered around a small stream. The rest stood as far away as they could get.

"Clay." One of the queasier agents, a warg from the looks of him, had spotted a lifeline. "Good to see you, man."

"Hey, Billy." He shook hands with him. "How'd you end up here?"

"I go where I'm told." He jerked his chin toward a man standing near the water. "You know how it is."

"I do." He waved to one of what must be the senior agents. "We better get in there."

While I had been kept isolated from other agents, for the most part, Clay had been a Black Hat forever. He knew everyone, and everyone knew him. He was a walking Bureau roster, which came in handy.

"Sure thing." He leaned around Clay to better see me. "I'm Billy Kidd, by the way."

"Rue Hollis." I declined the hand he offered me. "The bodies are over there?"

"Yeah." To save face, he raked that same hand through his hair. "It's brutal."

"I can handle it."

Eager as a puppy to please, he kept chatting. "What do you think they'll call this guy?"

"Copycat." I watched his face fall. "He doesn't deserve more recognition than that."

No serial killers deserved glorified monikers that praised and popularized their depravity.

Clay hung back to check on the other guys, who were all green around the gills, but Asa followed me.

"You two didn't exchange pleasantries." I cut him a look. "You're not a team player?"

"The others are afraid of me," he said matter-of-factly. "It's easier if they pretend they can't see me."

"Those sweet, sweet children," I crooned in my best wicked witch voice. "Raised to believe if they ignore the monster under their bed, it won't get them." I smiled at him. "I don't care if their eyes are shut when I grab their ankles, do you?"

Lumping us together smoothed a subtle tension from his shoulders I hadn't noticed he carried until now.

"I thought you were dead." My old nemesis swept his gaze over me. "What are you doing here?"

"Same as you, Marty." I kept a pleasant expression on my face. "I'm working this case."

"I thought the only way out of Black Hat was in a pine box."

"That's what you get for thinking," I said sweetly. "Do you mind? I'm here to do a job."

The other senior agents struck me as vaguely familiar, but I couldn't put a name to them. They took their cues from Marty and gave me dead-eye stares that dared me to get in their way.

Asa they ignored as if he weren't standing at my elbow, which blew my mind.

Just because I was a girl, I was less scary? Really? I mean, I wasn't all that scary now, but I used to be.

"Báthory," one of the guys breathed as his eyes rounded to the size of softballs.

The others flinched at the name and took a healthy step back, reminding me of the good old days when I struck terror into the hearts of my coworkers. Except those days weren't all that great. It felt that way at the time, but the true high came from using black magic. I had to admit, I didn't miss people being afraid of me.

Much.

"I would prefer you never speak that name within my hearing again," I said coolly. "Step aside, please."

Between Mr. Big Mouth blabbing my surname, and the bomb Clay would drop on their heads about who was now in charge, I doubted we'd hear another peep from the agents for the duration of the case. They would open the emails from us as lead team, file their paperwork to look good for the director, but sit in their hotel rooms watching porn or sports, eating pizza, and waiting for their free ride to be over.

The agents scattered before I got within touching distance, and I got my first look at the crime scene.

A narrow but deep creek ran through its center, and the victims had been posed on a rocky outcropping. I was glad for Clay's suggestion I pack waders. They had saved me on the muddy hike down and would keep me dry while I conducted my examination.

The single similarity, as far as I could tell, between this killer and the Silver Stag was right in front of me.

The Stag had chosen fae girls between the ages of ten and eighteen, with healthy amounts of magic. The transformative spell was easier for him to cast and more likely to stick that way. He preferred his victims on four legs rather than two, and he had a thing for deer. Each time he completed a herd of four, he let them go. That is to say, he unpenned them. Then he hunted them down with a crossbow.

The Stag had been a black witch, but he practiced a type of magic even my ancestors found distasteful.

Rather than eating hearts to increase his power, he consumed souls.

To transform the girls, he drew their essence to the surface and fashioned the shape he wanted from it. The end result was a silvery-white spectral animal of his choosing. And when he pierced its heart with a silver-tipped arrow, the spirit parted from the flesh, allowing him to inhale it using a thrice-cursed spell.

These girls were still deer, their fur still white, and magic had frozen a tableau straight out of a painting.

A Spring Creek, the artist might name it, to highlight the vitality of the flowers on the shore and the rush of water that lent the arrangement a sense of movement. Even their eyes gleamed, bright and alert.

There were no wounds, defensive or otherwise, on the deer. They appeared well-fed, with sleek coats. It occurred to me he might have brushed them postmortem. He had taken care of the herd, but I wasn't as convinced he had hunted them. In addition to the cleanliness of their fur, no mud caked their hooves. The creek explained how the killer washed them but not how he got them here.

The average whitetail doe weighed about a hundred pounds, and that was the nearest comparison here.

"The killer had to lift each deer individually and pose them," I murmured. "That was after the hunt."

"Yes," Asa said, startling me.

Lost in deciphering the grim scene, I hadn't noticed him follow me into the creek. "He's strong."

Even if he carried them in versus flushed them out, what he had done required great physical strength.

"Powerful too." I curled my fingers into my palm to keep from touching the nearest lifelike deer to taste the dark magic trapped like dander in her fur. "The MO is different, flashier—the copycat wants us to find his work and admire it—but the manner of death..." I could see why they wanted my opinion. "These girls were transformed using the same magic, if not the same spell the Silver Stag used, and their souls were consumed as well."

Four girls had been taken, according to the report, but I only counted three deer.

"Where's number four?" I raised my voice to include Asa. "The file didn't indicate one was missing."

"You won't get a word out of Agent Montenegro." Billy had worked up the nerve to approach me without Clay. "He's the strong, silent type."

Asa wasn't the only one who got protective of his teammates. "What does that make you?"

"The opposite?" He ruffled his short hair. "I heard you ask about the fourth girl."

Most everyone here came with supernatural hearing, so it came as no surprise they were listening in.

Still annoyed for the slight to Asa, I stared a hole through the warg. "And?"

"Her remains were found in a meat processing plant down the road." He swallowed hard. "Ma'am."

"That's not part of his ritual." I would have remembered that gory detail. "This is the first time."

And the killer was male, that much I could tell from his magical signature.

"This is a heavily hunted area," Kidd ventured. "A hunter might have just taken a statue."

"They're not statues." I smoothed the bite in my voice. "They're victims. Not lawn art."

"Cut him some slack." Clay's wide hands landed on my shoulders. "He's still learning to cope."

Humor did it for some people. Dissociation worked for others. This guy had chosen door number two.

As young as he looked, he had been with Black Hat longer than Asa's seven years to not be the newbie.

"If you figure it out," I told Kidd, "you let me know."

The agent, braver with Clay present, spilled the rest of the details.

"The owner came in to work this morning and found a mound of ground meat left half in the grinder. He was pissed off thinking his son got drunk and went hunting with his 'crazy ass wife'. But when he started cleaning up the mess, he noticed bone showing through. He went to scoop it in the trash and ended up palming a human skull packed in ground meat like one of those giant burgers with melting cheese centers."

"The killer involved humans." A story like that would grow legs. "That explains the number of agents."

The director wanted this killer stopped before he made a public exhibition of his art.

"He's escalating," Clay agreed. "The director won't let this stand."

"He consumes their souls." Asa watched water run over his boots. "Do you think he's eating their flesh too?"

"I doubt it." I studied the deer again. "There's no artistry in how those remains were found."

Steaks cut with the precision of a master butcher then wrapped in paper and tied with twine. I could see that. Neat stacks in the fridge, fresh and ready for pickup, a name in bold, black marker. That fit the theme too.

With a slap on the back, Clay sent the agent away. "Black witches don't practice both disciplines, right?"

"You're either *cridhe* or *anam*." A heart eater or a soul eater. "Eat the heart at its freshest and most powerful, and the soul ascends before you contain it. Consume the entire soul, and the heart is cold when you're done. Most, if not all, of its magic has dissipated by then." Aware it cast a spotlight on me, I told them the rest. "That's not to say a witch can't supplement his or her diet for a power boost outside their norm. Some do, some don't. Some flip back and forth, like vegetarians to veganism."

"I never thought I would hear eating hearts compared to eating hearts of romaine."

Knowledge of the black arts was a reason, not *the* reason, I had been hunted down and bribed to return. I had an inkling of what the other or others might be, but I had a contract to protect me from the worst of my suspicions.

"The processor was for show," I decided. "A human skull, right? The fourth girl wasn't transformed."

"We won't know until we receive the autopsy results." Asa lifted his head. "Dr. Lennon has to determine if the remains were fae, then crosscheck the skull DNA against the ground meat. If it's a match, she has to run tests to compare those results with the samples we have on file for the fourth girl."

"This part of the job hasn't changed while I was away, huh? It's waiting, waiting, and more waiting."

"The results come quicker now." Clay chided my impatience. "There have been several breakthroughs in the last ten years on the magic side that allows faster processing and guarantees more accurate results."

"I look forward to being amazed."

One of the first skills a novice witch learned was how to sew. The talent lent itself to medical, ritual, and practical applications. I had taken to sewing a long, slender pocket into all my pants to store my wand on trips. The access point was no larger than a standard buttonhole, barely noticeable, and I learned how to sit just so in order to conceal the hard length running down my thigh. I reached for my wand now.

"I need three volunteers good for holding a hundred pounds on the hike back to the SUVs."

"As if you had to ask," Clay muttered then elbowed Asa. "We've got two covered."

"Yes," Asa said quietly. "We can transport two of the girls."

Kidd splashed back to us when no one else budged to lend a hand.

"I can't do it alone," he said, eyeing my first two volunteers, "but Taylor over there can help me."

Clay singled out the other junior agent. "Taylor looks ready to faint."

"You sure he's up for it?" He did seem pukey to me. "I don't want her dropped when we hit the incline."

"I'll do it."

Everyone on the shore turned to gawk at Asa.

"The girls will be safe with me."

"Thanks." I touched his arm then singled out the brave junior agent who had showed more backbone, or maybe more heart, than his peers combined. "When I break the spell, the girls will go limp. I don't want the third one to fall in the water. Can you and your friend hold her steady until Asa can lift her?"

The crestfallen agent waved over his friend. "Absolutely."

"You two brace the girl on the lowest rock." It was the easiest job, but I didn't want to ding their pride. "I worry about her sliding into the water the most."

On his way to brace the middlest girl, Clay whispered in my ear, "Softie."

For that, I briefly considered turning him into a frog, but I needed every ounce of magic at my disposal.

The final girl, the one placed at the highest and most difficult spot, fell to Asa due to his shifted height.

I joined the girls on the rocky outcropping since magic and running water didn't play nice. Wand in hand, I began the counterspell to unravel the gossamer filaments holding them in place. Each word cost me to speak, a reminder I was not what I used to be, but I finished without faltering and felt the cords break.

I didn't remember closing my eyes, but I opened them to find a familiar daemon across from me with his limp burden on one shoulder. I didn't notice I was staring until Clay cleared his throat. I pretended not to catch his meaning and checked on the two junior agents. They were holding steady, but poor Taylor was pale as bleached bone. An oddly high-pitched noise escaped Taylor's throat when Asa crouched next to us to make transferring the girl onto his empty shoulder easier.

A whine, I realized, making me wonder if he was a warg too. No wonder those two stuck together.

"You guys head on up." I studied the empty rock. "I need to cleanse this place before we go."

"You heard her." Clay set out. "Come on, Ace."

The daemon watched me until he was forced to break eye contact, but he showed his duty the respect it deserved. I was left alone with Kidd and... "What was your name again?"

The junior agent swayed on his feet. "David Taylor."

"Rue Hollis." I gave him a short nod then faced Kidd. "You better help your friend here to your ride."

"Are you sure you want to be alone?" He scanned the bank. "I doubt the killer stuck around but..."

The killer was an exhibitionist. His audience gave him the thrill. His art meant nothing without patrons.

There was no doubt in my mind he had been here, somewhere, when the Black Hats first arrived to soak up their reactions. He would view them as a critique on his work, which could make him that much more dangerous if he felt we failed to show proper appreciation.

"I can take care of myself," I assured him, though it was a lie. "I'll be up in a minute."

The longer the others believed I was a black witch, the safer I would be from those with a score to settle.

Once I was alone, I took a vial from my kit, unstoppered it, and sprinkled its contents on the rocks while I hummed a low song of mourning to cleanse the residual negative energies of the space. The running water would help the process along, but I didn't want to risk another dryad incident from contaminating the area.

The whole process took maybe fifteen minutes, and it left me winded from the effort. Sweat ran into my eyes and glued my shirt to my spine. The others might think I had decided to go for a swim at this rate. It was one thing to go into this knowing I was less than I once was, but another to experience the shortfall.

"Are you finished?"

I didn't startle at the voice. I was too tired for that. I think, maybe, I had expected to hear it.

"Yes," I panted, sloshing toward Asa where he stood on the shore. "Can I ask you a question?"

"Ask," he said, which guaranteed he would listen but didn't promise me an answer.

How very fae of him.

"The junior agents were huddled together as far from the scene as they could get." I hated to show what I considered weakness in that I had been clueless about the problem. "The scene was picturesque, if you didn't know what you were looking at, so why the revulsion?"

A softening in his expression warned me I wouldn't like what he had to say, but I needed to hear it.

"The black magic made them ill, mentally and physically." He hesitated. "You didn't notice?"

"No." It sucked having my suspicions confirmed. "Not until I began the counterspell."

The strands clung to my skin, tacky like cobwebs, rather than sliding off as they had back when I radiated the same negative energy. Then I had repelled black magic. Now it appeared I was vulnerable, to a degree, but not precisely sensitive to it. I had spent too long mired in darkness for it to register, and that was a dangerous liability to discover on my first day back.

The dryad must have been right about me. I still reeked of black magic. I should have known when Marty minded his manners instead of calling me out in front of everyone on my change in diet, and in power.

"How good is your poker face?" I watched for his reaction. "Did it bother you?"

"I was aware of it." He helped me up onto the bank. "It reminds me of home."

"You were raised...?" I checked behind us once more. "Or is that too personal?"

"I was raised by my fae mother." He started walking. "After my daemon father raped her."

The taste of foot soured my mouth as I fell in step with him. "I'm sorry."

"That he abused her or that she kept me?"

This conversation had taken a nosedive, and I lacked the skills to right its trajectory.

"That was rude of me," he said softly. "You've never treated me..."

...like a monster.

"I get it." I pushed out a sigh as we started to climb up to the SUV. "I didn't know how to act today. Aloof and all-powerful or polite and reasonably sure I wouldn't blow us all up unraveling that spell."

He made a thoughtful sound low in his throat.

"I'm safer if the others think I'm still a badass, but I'm not."

Though my actions would out me eventually, I considered cultivating my stink by wearing a few charms.

"You chose a path few witches in your position would have dared. Fewer still would be walking it ten or more years later with no signs of withdrawal." He used a sapling to haul himself up the last few feet. "Be proud of who you've chosen to be. Not many people embrace change even after they acknowledge their wrongdoing."

"Change is hard," I confessed. "I almost caved, with the dryad."

"I shouldn't have tempted you." He hesitated. "The daemon form you've seen is me at my most primal." He helped me up to level ground. "We're not separate, exactly, but we're not the same either."

"I wondered."

I almost mentioned the smoothies, but he had confided things of a deeply personal nature just now. The last thing I wanted to do was draw attention to what might be instinctive behavior and step in it again so soon after my earlier faux pas. Working alongside a variety of different species required making concessions.

As much as I loved my smoothies, I was willing to share them now and then if it helped put him at ease.

"I was about to send out a search team," Clay boomed as he strode over to us. "What took so long?"

"I'm out of practice." I rubbed my arms, recalling the tacky sensation of webs. "Or out of juice."

"You'll get the hang of it." He swung a heavy arm around my shoulders. "I'm proud of you."

We walked to our SUV, the last one remaining, and I was grateful when Clay held the door open for me.

"I'm beat." I slid down in my seat and shut my eyes. "I need to nap off that counterspell."

Food worked best to replenish my power, but a raw steak on the hotel tab would raise eyebrows. Sleep was the next best cure. Weary as I was from the spells I had cast, I could face-plant in my pillows and not twitch until morning. Lunch on the flight was an eternity ago, but I wasn't hungry. For food.

"We'll head to the hotel," Clay announced from the back, "eat dinner, and rest up for tomorrow."

"I'm down for part one and three. I'm going to beg off dinner. I'm too tired to be good company."

"We requested a connecting room." Asa flicked his gaze toward me. "To make it easier for us to come and go for meetings in your room." He smiled, just a little. "We gave you the suite."

"Nice." I settled in. "I haven't had a good soak in ages."

The tub and shower combo at my house barely covered my navel when I filled it to the top.

"Looks like it's you and me, Ace." Clay patted his partner on the shoulder. "Where do you want to eat?"

"I noticed a steakhouse past the airport," he suggested. "Or a twenty-four-hour diner near the hotel."

"The diner works for me." Clay sat back and rubbed his stomach. "I love all-you-can-eat pancakes."

Pretty sure he could eat them out of ingredients if he set his mind to it. Goddess knows he had plenty of times in the past. Once the free refills began to raise eyebrows, though, he tended to pay the bill, tip the waitress, and make his exit before management got involved while also hanging on to the receipt to remind himself not to hit the same place twice in one trip.

While the guys cemented their plans for the night, I let my thoughts drift and my power slumber.

I dreamed of counting sheep that leapt over stones and splashed down into a creek.

Somewhere along the line, the fluffy white sheep became sleek does with glossy eyes that didn't blink.

8

Faint knocking lifted me out of my deep sleep, and I jerked awake to find myself in a hotel room.

"Colby called Clay," Asa said through the door. "She's worried about you."

"What time is it?" I craned my neck until I spotted the alarm clock. "Midnight."

"I thought you would want to know."

Muffled steps retreated before I could thank him. Fumbling my muted phone out of my pocket, I dialed Colby, who hit video chat, bringing her adorable face into full view.

"You didn't call," she accused. "You didn't return mine either."

"I had a rough first day. I'm sorry." I shoved upright. "I should have called you before I crashed."

"You should have." Her antennae stood on end. "I worried about you."

"I'll tell Clay if I ever wipe out on the job, it's his duty to call you to let you know I'm okay."

"I'm not happy with you." She used her mocking tone, aka her impression of me. "You know better."

"Okay, twerp, you're pushing it." I chuckled. "I said I was sorry, and I meant it."

"It better not happen again."

"It won't." I crossed my heart. "I have learned from my mistakes and vow never to repeat them."

I gave her a second to enjoy calling me out, which was deserved, before I returned the favor.

"It's midnight here." I spied her computer screen blazing. "What time is it there?"

"I couldn't sleep." She made her eyes bigger and rounder. "I had to know you were okay first."

"Aww." I mimed wiping a tear. "Now go to bed."

"This is the thanks I get for worrying."

"Night-night."

"Sleep tight."

"Don't let the bedbugs bite."

The call was the exact medicine I needed to get back to one hundred percent. Feeling guilty, I texted Asa an apology for Colby bothering them. Clay didn't sleep, but he zoned out to binge shows on his phone. It was my fault both of them were wide awake and plugged in at this hour.

>>*You didn't interrupt us. We're going over the pictures from today.*

>*I'm wide awake now. Want to come over?*

Rereading it—after I hit send, of course—I cringed.

>*To work?*

>>*We'll gather the files and join you.*

The guys had left me in my clothes, which meant I only had to roll out of bed to be ready.

Clay, I wouldn't have minded undressing me. Bodies were bodies. As far as he was concerned, I had nothing new or interesting to see. Plus, when we worked together, we often posed as a couple and shared a room. He had seen it all, many times, and didn't give a fig.

But Asa...

He was complicated in a way I didn't need or want right now. Maybe ever. He had baggage, a full set. Just like me. He probably had a history that would turn human hair white. Also like me. Otherwise, he wouldn't be in Black Hat.

I didn't understand Asa's cultures well enough to grasp if his interest was reciprocal, or if his possessive tendencies came with the dominant daemon package.

And it was a nice package.

I really had to stop thinking about his package.

For a split second before the door between rooms swung open, I entertained taking a cold shower.

"Hey, Dollface." Clay carried three black bags to the table. "How's Coco?"

Still fuzzy around the edges, I squinted at him. "Coco?"

"Colby?" He snorted. "She needs a nickname, so I don't slip up in front of the wrong people."

Not a bad idea, and it warmed me that he hit her with a nickname so fast, whatever his reasons.

"Mad." I rolled a shoulder. "I missed our chat time."

We scheduled it before I left, to be sure we kept up with one another while I was away.

"I told her you had to be carried in." Clay shook his head. "Guess that didn't make a dent."

"Nope." I claimed a chair. "Can I ask you a favor?"

"Name it." He unpacked three laptops and shoved them into position. "What do you need?"

A pinch in my chest reminded me why I had missed this, missed *him*, so much.

Clay might not technically be a person, but he was good people.

"Can you call Colby if this happens again? Just let her know I'm okay, and I'll be in touch later?"

"Is that all?" He snorted. "Done."

Asa carried an armload of junk food and dumped it on the table. "I brought snacks."

The crinkle of a potato chip bag set my stomach grumbling. "Bless you, kind sir."

"I told him what you like." Clay shot his partner a narrow-eyed stare. "You should thank me."

"Thank you, other kind sir." I swatted his arm. "What's with the territoriality?"

"You know how it is." Clay finished setting up and sat gingerly in his chair. "Daemons will be daemons."

"I don't know how it is or even what that means." I selected a computer. "I assume that was the point?"

"There's no denying my daemon side is intrigued by you," Asa said smoothly. "It worries Clay."

There was a world of difference between Asa telling me *he* was interested versus his daemon.

"You don't sound concerned." I opened a bag of chips and popped one in my mouth. "Should I be?"

"I won't harm you, no." He hesitated. "Neither will the daemon."

If Clay had been sucking on a lemon, he couldn't look sourer. "Just know I'm watching you, Ace."

A slow smile spread Asa's full lips, and he dipped his chin in an oddly respectful gesture. "I'm aware."

"Unless you guys plan on getting less cryptic," I griped and crunched, "we might as well get to work."

The password on my computer of choice was the same one Clay always used, which was all kinds of bad. These laptops contained data that could rock the human world if one was discovered and hacked. As far as passwords go, *123ABC* was downright pathetic. That prompted me to ask, "Is this one yours?"

"What's mine is yours." He laughed when my eyebrows slammed down. "It's new, okay? It's for you."

Now that he mentioned it, it did have that new circuit board smell.

"What were you guys looking at before Colby interrupted?"

"Maps." Asa turned his laptop around, which already had a tab open with three red dots pinned to a digital map of the area. "The crime scenes are within twenty-five miles of one another."

"You think the killer is local?" I went through the motions of setting up the laptop how I liked it. "There's another common thread, right? The properties where the victims have been found are off logging roads. The areas are in the process of being clear-cut."

"That fits with him being local." Clay left his laptop shut. "He could be scouting locations on the job."

Done futzing, I asked, "How many logging companies operate within a fifty-mile radius of Asheville?"

"A lot." Clay snorted as he peeked over Asa's shoulder. "A quick search pulls up twenty-five."

"So, we find out which companies had contracts for each kill site, get a copy of their employee rosters, and see if we have any match-es." For companies, employees, or hopefully both. "Are the Kellies still in research?"

"They'll be glued to screens until they die," Clay said fondly. "And love every minute of it."

Arthur Kelley and Kelly Angelo—aka the Kellies—were the Black Hat research team.

Arthur was an old-as-dirt vampire, Kelly was a fledgling gargoyle, and they were as head over heels with the job as most folks were for their mates. With their light sleep schedules, the pair worked pretty much around the clock. Neither were allowed outside the Black Hat compound. The security feeds allowed the two a view of the changing world without risking human lives by releasing them into it.

"Do we have video of the scene?" I wasn't up to speed on current procedure. "Or is that old school?"

"First on scene films it," Clay confirmed. "We have vest cams now too, but the director nixed them for this case."

"I'll put in a request." Asa clicked a few keys. "We'll have it in the morning."

"He didn't want to risk a leak." Smart move on his part. "One video is easier to suppress than ten."

"That supports our concerns that the killer will take his, to borrow from Rue, *art* public." Asa frowned. "I wonder if there's a secondary reason for the director's precautions within the Bureau."

"An inside man?" Clay tilted his head. "I wouldn't rule it out."

"The Silver Stag files were sealed as soon as we realized we had a serial killer," I recalled. "An agent back then might have heard gossip around the office. Now, aside from the personal notes of those involved, it would require express permission from the director to access that case."

The question wasn't *if* one of our fellow agents was capable of committing this Stag-worthy crime spree. That answer was a resounding *yes*. But if it was one of our own, then why wait a decade? Why the Stag?

"For now," I decided, "I'm going to chalk the director's behavior up to an overabundance of caution."

"You don't like the idea of sizing a fellow agent for a noose?"

Glancing up from the screen, I found Asa watching me with steady intent. "Not particularly."

Most of us had done the crime and the time. Punishment ought to end at some point, in my opinion. But Black Hat was a lot like the mob. Marty was right about one thing. The only sure way to leave the Bureau for good was in a pine box.

"We're veering off track." Clay rapped his knuckles on the table. "Logging companies are a good place to start. The Kellies can have that information to us first thing. We'll follow that lead from there."

I could have contacted the Kellies myself, but I wasn't ready to talk without hexing them yet.

They sniffed out intel for agents working cases, yeah, but that was a drop in the bucket of their duties.

The duo also tracked prey for the director via the internet.

Prey that now included me.

The Kellies had been doing their jobs. More importantly, they had no choice *but* to do their jobs.

I knew that. I did. I understood. Sympathized even. We were all trapped. Caged within the Bureau's bars. True, the world was safer with us contained, *leashed*. But through me, they had put Colby in the director's crosshairs, and that I had trouble forgiving.

"Works for me." I had another thought. "Do we know if the truckers are employed by the company? Or are they independent contractors?"

"I'll make a note," Asa murmured. "The Kellies can dig up that information while they're at it."

A familiar trilling sent me in search of my cell, which I had left on the bed. "Hello?"

"The wards blinked just now."

Ice glazed my spine, and my fingers curled around the phone. "As in contact?"

The wards had a few different indicators I rigged for Colby, who couldn't feel them the way I did when in close proximity. The most common was a blink, which meant that a person or object had made contact. I had the sensitivity dialed all the way up while I was away, which meant anything bigger than a chipmunk would trigger a blink.

The blink itself was conveyed via a decorative traffic light I mounted on the wall above Colby's monitor. I fixed it so brief contact with the wards would flash yellow for caution. Prolonged contact turned it red. If all was well, it remained green.

"It was yellow," she said in a tiny voice. "It's okay, I'm okay, I just wanted you to know."

"Keep an eye on it." We both knew she wasn't going to sleep any time soon without adult supervision. "Tell me if it goes red, and I'll be on the next flight home."

"Okay," she said softly. "Call me in the morning?"

"You got it." I let her hang up then opened the security app on my phone. "Better safe than sorry."

The guys, who had no trouble overhearing private conversations, would guess at my panic.

The first thing I did after purchasing the house was blanket it with security cameras. I wanted a warning to come through to us even if my wards unraveled before they sounded an alarm. I was doubly grateful for that paranoia now, as I flipped from camera to camera, bouncing from the porch view to the various entry points to the empty driveway and then to the tree mount that overlooked the entire house.

"I don't see anything." I exhaled through my parted lips. "It was probably an animal."

"There are plenty of rabbits, deer, raccoons, foxes, and smaller prey on and around your property."

The rundown from Asa, who had hunted there, made me feel better. However, Clay was unamused for it to come to light that Asa had been on the prowl while he was paralyzed and had chosen my property for his hunt.

"I get alarms if the camera perimeter is breached," I told them, "but I'll turn on motion alerts too."

"Maybe we should call it a night." Asa noticed the time. "It's been a long day."

"That sounds good." I set down my phone. "I'll shower and order room service while you rest."

"I can stay if you want company." A wrinkle pinched Clay's brow. "I can binge *Baketopia* later."

"That reminds me…" I squared off against him. "Your addiction to baking competitions is the reason why I stress bake. I hope you know that." I jabbed a finger into his hard abs, which had literally been sculpted to perfection. "I could have opened a bakery with all the flour, butter, and sugar I've gone through in the last decade all because you got me hooked on sweets."

Yet another reason he booked suites. They tended to come with full—if mini—kitchens. If he got bored with streaming videos or reading on his phone late at night, he got out of bed and hit Pinterest for recipes.

One night, early into our partnership, when my dreams were extra gruesome, Clay invited me to join him at the stove. The rest was history.

"I could have groceries delivered while you shower." He winked. "I still remember that cookie recipe."

"Kitchen sink cookies." I wiped my mouth in case I drooled. "Can we bake them tomorrow night?"

"Sure thing." He grinned. "I'll get an order together. I expect we'll be here another day at least."

"That sounds perfect." I flipped a hand at the equipment. "You guys can leave that here."

"Okay." Clay led the charge back to their room. "See you in the morning, Dollface."

Asa was slower to follow, and he paused on the threshold between rooms to toy with my doorknob.

"We left this unlocked earlier." He twisted the deadbolt. "I would rectify that."

That wasn't worrisome to hear right before bed. "You carried me in, right?"

Hand sliding off the door, he lowered his gaze. "I did."

"Then thank you." I joined him on the threshold, placed my hand on his chest, and pushed. "Night."

After I shut the door between us, I heard a faint exhale that sounded like "Good night."

9

I ordered in breakfast before I called the guys and invited them to my suite for updates. It was the least I could do to make up for last night. I still felt bad about Colby disturbing them to reach me, but I felt even worse for neglecting her. This was our first time apart, and I was falling down on the job on day one.

Yes, circumstances beyond my control were to blame.

No, that didn't matter one bit to a scared kid home alone.

A kid who must have stayed up all night playing with her friends if she was missing her requested call.

This time, I would leave a message to make sure she knew I hadn't forgotten about her.

"You're not answering, so I assume you're unconscious. Call if you need me. Or if you need anything. You're good on food, right? Enough sugar water to last you? How about snacks? Do you need—?"

A knock on the room dividing door kept me from going overboard with the helicopter parenting.

Or not.

Ending the embarrassingly long voicemail, I opened the security app on my phone and jumped indoor cameras until I spotted Colby asleep in her chair in front of her computer. Safe and sound.

Another knock had me rushing over to twist the lock and let the guys in. "Morning."

"Do I smell bear claws?" Clay sniffed as he entered the room. "Did you knock over a bakery?"

A smile twitched in my cheek when I noticed a gleaming black pompadour perched on his head.

"Those are apology muffins and bear claws of remorse. There's also coffee of forgiveness and milk of..." I thought about it. "Okay, I'm not sure what the milk signifies, but it's whole milk. Your favorite."

"How about 'milk of you didn't have to do this'?" He sat and claimed a bear claw. "You're a package deal with Colby. We knew that when we left Samford."

The rich tobacco scent I had come to associate with Asa filled my nose as he entered the room.

He wore his Black Hat suit but had left his hair down, and it flowed in a smooth sheet past his hips. His septum bling was a thick silver barbell, and his earrings tiny dots to match. I briefly wondered if he was pierced elsewhere, but I couldn't focus, even on dirty thoughts, past the hair.

The girly girl in me craved to plait it. Like my fingers actually curled in want of a brush. An overwhelming *need* to touch it made my palms itch. He was lucky I didn't have any hairbands on me. Otherwise, I might have attacked him with an insatiable lust to style him.

"Morning," he said softly. "How did you sleep?"

"Better than I have in years." That was the honest truth. "I was too tired to toss and turn."

A quick turkey club from the hotel kitchen, which cost twenty-five dollars, made for a decent meal. After I showered the woods and creek off me, I expected to stare at the ceiling until dawn. The earlier nap had been glorious, and I didn't expect to get lucky twice in one night. With the Sandman, that is.

The jerk had been holding out on me *forever*, so I was thrilled he felt like putting out for a change.

"You bought breakfast." He took the seat opposite mine. "That was thoughtful."

"The call," Clay explained between bites. "This is edible guilt."

After careful consideration of his options, Asa claimed a muffin. He also poured himself a black coffee.

With my guests both eating, I sat and selected a muffin. To play the game well, I chose one with a similar blueberry to crumble ratio. I couldn't help myself. It was a compulsive behavior at this point. Part of me had to know what Asa would do. I had a good idea, of course, but I had no idea *why* he did it. That smidgen of mystery was enough to convince myself I ought to yank the daemon's tail.

Not that Asa had a tail. That I had seen. Did he, though?

Hmm.

"I got a present in my inbox." I pulled up the file from the Kellies. "I assume you both received a copy?"

"The crime scene recording." Clay sounded about as thrilled as me to view it. "Synchronize watches."

"Hitting play..." I hovered my finger over the key, "...now."

The first five minutes made me regret the one bite of muffin I had taken to mark it.

"I can't see a thing." Clay rubbed his stomach like the jumpy footage also made him queasy. "Too blurry."

The agent wasn't walking at a fast clip so much as he was sliding down the embankment, which made for a tilt-a-whirl ride for his viewers. Namely us. His arm steadied when his feet hit the flat bottom, and I got my first look at the untouched crime scene.

The camera panned a slow circle, taking in the surroundings, before the agent advanced to the creek. He paused there, stood on the bank, and filmed the three lifelike does posed on the rocky outcropping. One sat with her legs tucked under her. Another stood tall and proud at the peak. The last victim balanced on three legs while the fourth leg hovered over the water, as if she were about to jump.

A sleek crow, perched on the highest doe's head, cawed for the camera before leaping into the sky.

The illusion was so convincing, had I come across this tableau on a hike, I would have frozen, breath held, for fear of spooking the deer.

The video progressed from there. The agent waded into the creek to film the rock from all angles and spent a long time on each doe to ensure no details were lost. When he finished, he backed onto the shore and ended the cut with another framed shot of the entirety of the killer's handiwork.

"Who filmed this?" I queued it to play again. "He did a good job."

"Billy Kidd." Clay read off his screen. "Credits are at the very bottom."

The word *credits* triggered a suspicion Billy might have been a film major in college.

"Nothing stood out to me." Asa drummed his fingers. "What are we looking for?"

"Anything." I was reminded of my conversation with Billy. "Kidd was hesitant to leave me alone at the scene after everyone else had headed back. He brought up a good point I should have considered sooner. That the killer would have been present when the first agent arrived to receive a critique of his work."

"You've been out of the game." Clay shrugged. "It'll come back to you."

"Kidd was right." Asa grew a scowl. "We should have thought of it and ensured you had backup."

"Rue is a badass." Clay reached for his milk. "She didn't need us babysitting her. It would have sent the wrong message to the other agents. It's better that we let her to do her thing, as per usual. We were a holler away, so it's not like she was in any real danger."

Except a well-aimed curse would have reached me quicker than they could have, and they both knew it.

Still, I appreciated Clay's usual thoughtfulness in helping me preserve the illusion of being all-powerful.

"The point is—" I waved a napkin as a white flag, "—the killer might be present in this footage."

"Nothing stood out." Asa leaned back in his chair. "We'll send it back to the Kellies with your theory."

They had the time, the tech, and the tenacity to ferret out any clues the killer might have left behind.

"That works." Clay used a pinky to gently navigate his keyboard. "Looks like the Kellies are putting in OT on this one. Check your inboxes, lady and gent. We've got confirmation the same lumber company held the contract for all three crime scenes. There's a list of truckers and machine operators, as well as other employees."

"They did the crosschecking for us." I grinned at that, half wishing I could hire the Kellies for minutia at Hollis Apothecary. "Looks like we've got a dozen employees present at all three scenes." I checked their home addresses. "All male, all local." I pulled up a map app on my phone. "We can hit maybe half these today. A few of the independent contractors have an hour-plus commute in their trucks."

Not that it mattered if you drove a sleeper truck with a bed and other amenities for long-haul jobs.

"We can cut that number." Asa rubbed a finger across his bottom lip. "Four employees are human."

Supernaturals tended to stick to themselves or their own kind, but humans made good minions.

We couldn't rule out human involvement until we had a firmer grasp on our black witch's identity.

"Let's keep them on the list but put them on the bottom." I made notes of the residences nearest to our hotel. "Do we call ahead, or do we risk rolling up on an empty house?"

My gut told me the killer would welcome us into his home, serve us tea and cookies, and tell us anything that might help the case. Minus his confession, of course. He was starving for praise, not stupid. But there remained a slim chance he would bolt if he thought we were closing in on him.

"We risk it." Asa checked with Clay. "We don't want to tip off the killer."

"I agree." Clay shoved the last muffin into his mouth. "These girls confirmed his timetable. We have two, maybe three days before he starts collecting again. Past that point, we have a week to find the girls alive before he calls with coordinates for his latest masterpiece."

"All right." I closed my laptop and stuck it in the bag Clay provided. "Let's get moving."

When Asa disappeared into their room, I assumed to grab equipment, I leaned over to inspect his muffin but found only a wrapper. Okay. No evidence to be found there. That left the one next to me. The one that should be mine. I palmed the muffin and rotated it a full circle, but nope. It was pristine. Not a single bite missing. Not a berry nibbled.

Sneaky daemon had sneaked my breakfast and switched it for his, which both excited me to be right and also made me extra special curious why he had fixated on my food. Before I could decide to ask outright, I intercepted a glare from Clay that would have vaporized me had he possessed laser eyebeams.

Asa emerged with his hair in braids, hands full of equipment, and set out for the SUV.

As I followed him to the parking lot, I decided I would ask how he got his part razor straight every time.

One day. Not anytime soon. I didn't want him to know I had the hots for his hair.

On the drive, I settled in to flip through the case files of previous victims, hoping to jog a memory.

"He's got a type." I cringed from looking at the photos. "That's for sure."

There he followed the Silver Stag's ideal, which meant the copycat had researched the Stag's victims.

"The names of the Silver Stag victims were released to the public after his death." By *the public*, I meant the supernatural public, not humans. "Our copycat wouldn't have had to look hard to find their details."

Colby could have been any one of these girls. She *had* been one of them.

"The other details were sealed," Clay reminded me. "Only the agents who worked the original case know how he killed his victims, and those files are sealed tighter than a jar of pickles."

"Perhaps that justifies the divergence from the original MO?" Asa cut me a sideways glance. "What if the killer followed the case in the news, collected every snippet, but assembled the big picture wrong?"

"That would explain why he took girls who fit the profile," Clay agreed from the back. "He pulled off the trick that earned the Silver Stag his nickname, but those details were leaked early on. The exact manner of death was kept under wraps, and the copycat got it wrong."

"Or he chose to go his own way." Asa's lips turned down. "Which would mean he's not a true copycat."

As much as I hated to ask, I had to know how divergent this copycat was in his methodology.

"There was no sign of sexual trauma on the Stag's victims. Do we know about the recent victims yet?"

Asa tucked his chin, but he didn't say a word. Clay, thankfully, answered for him.

"The previous victims showed no signs of abuse."

"Small mercy." I stared out the window. "That was all the dignity he left them."

DNA would help the lab identify each girl. Their remains were cremated afterward to insulate the family from the harsh truth there was no return to normalcy for their daughters, even in death. An urn was the lesser of two evils, according to the director, and for once, I had to agree with him.

No parent ought to witness their child reduced to the trophy the killer made of them.

"This is it." Asa flicked on the blinker. "Our first suspect lives in this subdivision."

The homes were older, but the yards were neat. Kids played outside, and dogs chased them.

In a word, it looked safe. Not at all like a killer might be hiding amongst these normal, everyday people.

But normal was the best camouflage of all.

"We're looking for two-thirty-three." Clay leaned forward. "It should fall on the right side."

Sure enough, we spotted the house and pulled into the drive behind a pickup swathed in camo decals.

On my walk to the house, I paused at the driver-side door to peer in the vehicle, and I noticed a gun rack mounted in the rear window. It didn't mean this guy was our killer. Probably half the trucks in this neighborhood had them too. Hunting was how a lot of people in rural areas kept their families fed.

Clay headed straight for the door, and I followed, with Asa trailing me.

"People react better to Clay," he explained when he noticed me taking stock of our positions.

Hindbrain was a funny thing. Prey species, like humans, got a tickle in the back of their minds that let them know when they were being hunted. They might not have natural predators, but they had plenty of supernatural predators that fed on them or off them.

Despite Clay's tough-guy exterior, and Asa's more subdued appearance, human brains picked up on signals their conscious minds missed and transmitted them to their bodies in the form of flight-or-fight reflexes.

It said a lot about me, none of it good, that Asa hadn't pinged on my radar as a threat.

I needed to reevaluate the pecking order if I wanted to keep breathing. I had to prick my ego, let it burst, then poke the deflated remains to determine how much power I still held and where I ranked magically.

Otherwise, one day I would pick a fight I couldn't win and lose in spectacular fashion.

Used to be that butting heads with me was like bringing a knife to a gunfight.

Now I worried it was like bringing a hot knife to a room temperature stick of butter.

We witches were famous for melting, after all.

The door swung open before Clay could knock, which had me searching for cameras out of habit.

"I'm Agent Kerr with the FBI." He kept his expression bland. "We'd like to ask you a few questions."

The twist on our identification meant Clay saw or heard a potential human within the dwelling.

"This ain't about child support, is it?" The man glared at me like I had brought Clay to hold him upside down and shake him until coins fell out of his pockets. "Tell that woman I'll pay it when I feel like it. I didn't want no kids. She did. Now she's got 'em. It's not my fault she's too good to work to pay for 'em."

His open hostility toward women meant I had to keep my mouth shut for us to get answers.

However, that didn't prevent me from whispering a spell to nudge his responses in the right direction.

Not a truth spell, exactly, more like a light compulsion to make him comfy enough to confide in us.

No wand or contact required. Just the way I liked it.

"That's a local matter," Clay assured him, his voice tight. "We're not here about that."

"Oh." He scratched his bellybutton through his threadbare shirt. "What's this about then?"

The way he shifted to block the door made it clear he didn't plan on letting us in. Or putting on pants. His boxers were plaid, holey, and made me wonder if it was too soon to ask for a raise. They were also the only thing he had on, other than his tee.

"The bodies of three girls were discovered near one of the sites where you work," Clay explained. "We came to ask if you saw or heard anything or noticed anyone acting peculiar."

"Three girls?" The color drained from his ruddy cheeks. "I got five girls myself."

Girls he had no interest in supporting, if his tirade was anything to go on, but the spell had loosened his tongue.

"Which site?" He snapped back from the shock quicker than a rubber band. "I work all over."

Clay rattled off the address from yesterday, and we watched the light bulb click for our machinist.

"I worked there, yeah. For three, maybe four days." He tugged on his earlobe. "Didn't hear a peep as I recall, but I wouldn't with the earplugs in. Don't remember seeing anything odd either. Just me and the same old guys doing the same old thing." He shrugged. "The lots blur after a while. Just a bunch of trees and dirt. All that changes is the address."

"Thank you for your time." Clay pasted on a good ol' boy smile. "We appreciate your help."

We kept silent until we piled into the SUV. As one, the guys looked to me for my opinion.

"He's not our guy." I set my laptop on my knees. "The spell nudged him, and he gave us nothing."

However, the effort gave me a headache. It would have cost me less if I used the wand, but I didn't want a repeat of the dryad incident, where he smelled black witch and fought when I attempted to touch him.

"He's a goblin." Asa stared up at the house. "They're naturally more resistant to magic."

"True." I waited until I held his attention. "Do *you* think he's our guy?"

"No." He waited a beat. "I dislike him, intensely, but he lacks the…"

"…stink of a black arts practitioner?" I huffed out a laugh. "You can say it."

Asa said no such thing.

"He doesn't have the juice." Clay came to his partner's rescue. "He barely gave me the tingles."

As a creature animated by magic, Clay sensed power in others. From experience, he had a decent gauge.

To practice the black arts, you didn't have to be a witch, only magically gifted. But we excelled at it.

Our killer, copycat or not, was skilled in a way that left me certain he was witchborn.

"Then we move on." I pulled up the next address. "Looks like it's about fifteen minutes from here."

On the drive over, Colby texted me proof of life, a photo of her stuffing her face with pollen granules. An orange sports bottle rested on the desk beside her, a kiddie cup verging on doll sized, full of sugar water. And I, to avoid making her feel babied, didn't mention I had spied on her while she slept. Like an overprotective creeper.

I showed the guys, who both smiled at their first glimpse of her rig, as she called her gaming station.

"Your familiar bond with Colby..." Asa juggled his words more carefully. "Is it functional?"

"It's set, or she wouldn't be here."

"Can you draw power from her?" He kept his tone light and accusation free. "Can she draw from you?"

"I've never tried, and to my knowledge, neither has she."

"You can ever only bond to one familiar."

"I'm aware."

"Yet you refuse to use yours for her intended purpose."

"And?"

"I wonder how you bear it," he said softly. "The constant temptation to take what you want."

"It almost sounds like you're asking if I saved Colby to punish myself."

"Maybe I am."

"Maybe you're right." His question echoed thoughts I'd had

myself, years after the fact. "Maybe she was the motivation I needed to finally screw up the courage to change. Maybe I didn't feel I deserved a fresh start, but I knew she did." I wet my lips. "Colby saved me every bit as much as I saved her. Except I had it easy. I killed the Silver Stag for what he did to her and the other girls. Colby, she had to save me from myself."

"Curiosity is the curse of my heritage," he said quietly. "Half my heritage, in any case."

Since he dug around in my past, I felt entitled to his. "How do you identify?"

"As dae." He smiled a bit. "There are a lot of us." He glanced at me. "Enough to form our own subrace."

"Dae." I mulled it over. "I like it."

Though he kept quiet, I sensed Clay thinking hard at me, and they weren't happy thoughts.

He and I had covered old ground too, but it had taken months of partnership, not days of acquaintance.

But Asa had Clay to vouch for him, and a fraction of my trust of Clay extended to Asa on that basis.

I wasn't jumping in with both feet with Asa. More like dipping my toes in the water.

No matter what Clay thought, or how loud he thought it.

10

The *oh crap* handle found its way back into my hand when Asa pulled onto a pockmarked dirt road.

"Grit your teeth," Clay suggested, "or they might bounce loose."

A tidy singlewide trailer sat at the end of the long drive on a patch of bright-green grass. The sharp edges of the lawn told me the homeowner had laid sod but only enough to create their own mini oasis. A car in pristine condition, a miracle considering the state of the road, sat in front of the small porch.

This time, Clay got his chance to knock, and he did so carefully, as we had been greeted by a storm door.

A plump woman in a cherry apron greeted us with a welcoming smile. "How can I help you?"

"We're looking for Dan Malone." Clay grinned right back, and she blushed. "Does he live here?"

"Danny?" She waved an oven-mitted hand. "He's my husband. Come on in. I have cookies."

The file mentioned Dan Malone was a lynx shifter, but it made no mention of a wife.

"I never say no to cookies, ma'am." Clay led the way after she opened the door. "They smell divine."

"They're my specialty." She dialed her cheer higher. "Danny! Darling, these folks are here to see you."

An older man with white tufts of wiry hair sticking out of his ears entered the living room.

"Rose." His sigh ended on a growl. "What have I told you about letting strangers in the house?"

"We never have company," she fussed. "It gets lonely out here, all by ourselves."

Expression softening on her, he hardened again as he looked us up and down, pausing on me. "What do you want?"

With a shifter nose, I probably stank to high heaven to him. "I'm Agent Rue Hollis with the FBI—"

"You're Black Hat, dear." His wife tittered. "I smell it all over you."

"Apologies, ma'am." Clay turned his grin back on her. "We can't be too careful."

Plenty of paras married normals, and those humans were often kept ignorant of our world for their own good. But there was something about Mrs. Malone that made my nape tingle.

"I understand," she assured him. "I just wanted to let you know you can speak freely."

As I made them wariest, and their focus zeroed in on me, I handled the questioning.

"Three bodies were discovered on a site under contract by Lawry Lumber. We're here to ask—"

A few things happened at once.

Mrs. Malone burst into flames.

Mr. Malone erupted into his lynx form.

And the cookies we had been promised began to weep icing tears.

"What in tarnation is that?" Clay recoiled, not from the paras, but from the cookies. "They're...*alive*?"

"I only take what I need," the column of flame that was Mrs. Malone crackled at us. "Just enough."

Mr. Malone braced his silver paws on the linoleum, barring us from the kitchen and his wife.

"Are you responsible for the deaths of three girls killed with black magic?" Asa stepped forward. "You're both hunters. I doubt you would stoop so low as that in order to feed."

"I don't harm children." Mrs. Malone's flames rose higher. "Who would do such a thing?"

"That's why we're here," Asa explained. "We're hunting their killer."

Since he didn't appear to be making much headway, I jumped in while Clay continued playing defense.

"Whatever you've done, we're not here for you." I included them both in my statement. "Either of you." I held up my hands. "All we want are answers about this particular case. Give those to us, and we'll go."

"All right." Mrs. Malone extinguished herself, leaving us with a soot-dusted and extremely naked old woman. "Danny, I think we should help them." She stroked his head. "Change back, please."

The lynx took a bit longer to shift without his mate in immediate danger. Mr. Malone stood, ready for a fight, and buck naked. A low growl pumped from his chest until his wife swatted at his arm with a laugh.

"He's so overprotective." She fluffed her smoking hair. "Stop fussing, and tell them what you know."

Her husband cleared his throat and singled me out yet again. "There were three sites, weren't there?"

Clay's fingers tightened into fists, Asa moved in closer to me, and I locked my knees to hold myself still.

"Yes," I confirmed. "How did you know?"

"I hunt on the tracts I work. I go late. After everyone's gone home." He rolled a bony shoulder. "It wasn't natural, those deer, so I let them alone." He tapped his nose. "I smelled the black magic on them."

Rude as it was of me, I had to ask, "Do you think you could follow the scent for us, see where it leads?"

"I tried then, when it was fresh, and had no luck." He watched my face and nodded to himself. "I stalked the trail, but it vanished within yards of the bodies each time. I would've killed him, if I could've sunk my claws in him. I knew Black Hats would come." He kissed his wife's cheek. "I knew you would find us."

One salient point stood out to me. "You're sure the black magic user was male?"

A second opinion never hurt, especially since I was still finding my balance.

"He marked his territory." Mr. Malone chuffed. "Guess he thought it would keep wildlife away. As if any animal would go near a place seeped in that much negative energy. The magic alone warns them off it."

From a shifter, that was as good as a positive ID in my book. "What do you mean by the trail vanished?"

"He doused it with diesel fuel from the site." He sneezed at the memory. "It clogged my nose something fierce when it was fresh. I went back a few days later, and all I smelled was fuel. He was smart to do it."

A few days later meant Mr. Malone had been first on scene and last on scene each time. He made a valuable resource.

"Smart unless someone dropped a match." Clay whistled. "I didn't see mention of that anywhere."

"Maybe city folk figure all clear-cutting sites stink like fuel." Mr. Malone shrugged again. "I can't speak to that. All I can tell you is what I saw and what I smelled each time."

"If you come across another scene, do us a favor and call it in, please." Asa handed him a business card. "That's my direct number. You can be an anonymous tipster."

"How exciting." Mrs. Malone clasped her hands. "It's just like on TV."

"We will protect your identities if you cooperate with us," Asa told her husband. "You have my word."

The old man flipped the card over his fingers. "And if I don't cooperate?"

Based on their initial reactions, I got the feeling the warning would hit harder coming from me.

"Then we dig into your wife's background and take a look at missing persons cases in the area." I let him see I meant every word. "We don't go out of our way to make trouble for folks who fly under the radar." I patted my pocket, where my wand resided. "Black Hat doesn't have to know about your wife, or you."

"I want a truth binding," he growled. "Give me that, and I'll cooperate."

Clay opened his mouth, ready to argue, but I didn't mind bleeding. "Done."

Behind me, Asa rumbled the faintest growl, but he didn't say a word. Smart move. He couldn't stop me.

The binding was a simple exchange of vows and blood, and it took all of five minutes.

Unfortunately for me, it drained every ounce of energy I had remaining to walk out of that trailer. Yet again, I had underestimated the cost active magic versus the passive magic I used in the store at home would charge me. But given how protective Mr. Malone was of his missus, I wasn't about to show weakness in front of predators of that caliber.

Back in the SUV, I melted into my seat and shut my eyes. "I hate putting the screws to people."

"But you're so good at it," Clay teased to brighten my mood. "He's an asset, and you secured his cooperation. The rest is the cost of doing business."

"I know, I know." I massaged my temples. "Toeing the company line and all that."

"So, Mrs. Malone." The SUV rocked as Clay settled in the back. "What's up with her?"

"She's a dragon." Asa didn't hesitate in his assessment. "Her powers are bound. Otherwise, she wouldn't have stopped with self-immolation. She would have transformed and, most likely, eaten us to protect herself and her mate."

"I was thinking phoenix," I admitted, "but those cookies..."

"Dragons eat people," he said simply. "Phoenixes do not."

"She was going to feed us people cookies?" Clay made a gagging noise. "That's so...*wrong*."

"They were crying." I remembered that now. "How is that possible?"

"Dragons have strange magic. I knew a dragon, years ago, who spelled his steaks to moo when he cut into them. It was quite the party trick when he invited guests over for a cookout."

"Are you telling me," I asked calmly, "she spelled her cookies to cry *as she ate them*?"

"As I said." Asa rubbed his thumb on the steering wheel. "Strange magic."

"Sounds more like strange, period," Clay grumbled, still miffed. "People cookies."

Unable to help myself, I teased, "People put bacon in cookies. That's meat."

"Chocolate, nuts, caramel, fruit—those belong in cookies."

Sadly, as funny as it was to wind up Clay, his rant worsened my blossoming headache.

"We can go back to the hotel," Asa offered, noticing my discomfort, "pick this up again tomorrow."

Mid-diatribe, Clay snapped his mouth shut and shifted his focus from baked goods abuse onto me.

"The next suspect is only about thirty minutes away." I flipped a hand. "Might as well hit him too."

"Asa and I can handle this one alone." Clay patted my head. "You can stay put."

"Maybe." An outright refusal would only spark an argument. "I'll think about it."

Thinking turned into another blasted nap that left me waking up alone in the SUV.

I had good reasons for giving up black magic, and it hadn't mattered at home, but in the field?

For a minute, I was sorely tempted to fall back on old habits to keep up with my teammates.

And, if I was being truthful, to feed the monster chained in the basement of my mind.

Only the knowledge I had to look Colby in the eye when I got home kept me honest.

I'm a white witch. I'm a white witch. I'm a white witch.

Not wanting to interrupt any rapport the guys might have established with the suspect, I checked emails and otherwise entertained myself while staying put. But thirty dull minutes later, when they still weren't back, I considered stretching my legs for a quick peek inside the rusting travel trailer that was the only structure for a few miles in any direction.

As I clutched the handle, the trailer's front door blew off its hinges and smacked into the windshield. The glass didn't break, but it spiderwebbed until there was no chance of us driving it anywhere else. Wand in hand, I exited the SUV and prepped a binding spell guaranteed to wipe me out for the rest of the day.

"Stand down," Clay hollered to me from inside the trailer. "We're good."

Ignoring the order, wand at the ready, I held my position.

The entire trailer rocked as a familiar daemon made his exit, careful not to inflict more damage. His right horn gave him problems, but he figured out the angle and leapt to the ground rather than use the stairs.

I was unsurprised when he made a beeline for me. However, I was surprised when he took a fistful of his hair and offered it to me. He shook it at me until I accepted it, and it was all I could do not to laugh at his earnest expression. Maybe I wasn't as smooth as I thought, and Asa had noticed me coveting his hair. Or if not him, his more primal self.

"You have very pretty hair." I ran it through my fingers. "Thank you for, um, sharing it with me."

That seemed to please him, and he stood sentry beside me, leashed by his hair, until Clay joined us.

Clay took one look at the handful of hair, shut his eyes, inhaled, exhaled, then ignored it altogether.

"That was the father of *a* missing girl." Clay gusted out a sigh. "I told him her disappearance didn't fit our timeline, that she wasn't one of the victims we found, and it pissed him off worse."

"He thought you had news." I saw the problem and sympathized with the guy. "He was hoping for closure."

"He punched the door." Clay eyeballed the battered SUV. "Guess you noticed."

As my adrenaline ebbed, I felt safe enough to pocket my wand, but I was stuck holding daemon hair.

I doubt they got much out of him, but I still asked, "Did he offer anything useful?"

"He said if we want to know about his daughter, we should check the missing persons reports he filed."

Believe me, I would do just that. "How certain are we she's not a previous victim?"

"Pretty sure since this guy wasn't flagged on the suspect list. The Kellies don't make mistakes often, but I would have handled the situation differently had I known. We need to update his file."

The timeline left me certain I was missing critical information. "What took so long?"

"That would be the twenty-minute standoff where he held a gun loaded with cold iron rounds at Ace." A grimness pinched his expression. "Ace believes he could have survived it, but he seems as fae as not to me. I didn't want to take any chances."

The daemon beside me grumbled under his breath as if to say *I beg to differ.*

I would have told him we were all more than the sum of our worst parts, but I wasn't convinced I believed it either.

"This is why you shouldn't ditch me." Clay *knew* better than to leave me behind. "I could have thrown a sleep spell at him."

Bart Olsen, according to his file, was a troll. Trolls were *highly* territorial. They tended to punch unexpected visitors in the face then let their guests announce themselves while spitting out teeth.

They also kept caches of various items of value. To them. Not necessarily to anyone else.

Yet another reason for their legendary aggression. They guarded their prized possessions to the death.

One troll on the company payroll built a fallout shelter to house his pickled foods hoard.

Carrots, pigs' feet, beets, green beans, eggs, okra, as well as a variety of the classic pickled cucumber.

Go figure.

"We could have thrown *you* at him." Clay chuckled at my temper. "You were dead to the world."

"Drool," the daemon beside me growled. "Everywhere."

With a handful of his hair, I did what came naturally. I yanked. Then I regretted my act of hair violence. It wasn't his hair's fault that the daemon was teasing me. His flowing locks were innocent. I owed them an apology.

"You can have this back." I pressed the hair into the daemon's hand. "I'm getting in the SUV."

Still chuckling, Clay leaned over to inspect the windshield, cursed, then punched his fingers through both ends and lifted it clear out of the frame. He stowed it in the trunk for disposal, solving the problem of how we planned on getting back to the hotel. Waiting for a tow truck in the yard of a grieving and violent parent must have appealed about as much to him as it did to me. Even if the modification to the SUV meant we arrived with bugs in our teeth.

With that task done, Clay climbed in while the daemon stood pouting with his hair in hand.

"You're playing with fire," Clay warned in a low voice. "That behavior ain't natural for Ace."

"It ain't natural for me either."

"I know," he sighed, settling back. "That's what worries me."

Leaning forward, I stuck my head through the windshield. "Are you driving or...?"

The transformation swept over Asa, flames racing across his body, leaving him standing in his pants.

There must be an elastic waistband in them that allowed the material to expand and contract. His shirts were fitted, though, and they never survived the transition. Not that I minded the view of the aftermath.

The noise drew the homeowner's attention, easy to do with his front door gone, and Asa stared at him.

"I have spare clothes," Asa said, eyes on the man in the doorway, "but I don't think it would be wise to linger."

"I'm inclined to agree with you." I didn't like the way Olsen was looking at us. "We should go."

Before he decided that a black witch on his property was the straw that broke...well...*my* back.

"Ace can handle driving with the windows down." Clay chuckled evilly. "Right, Ace?"

Asa got behind the wheel, cranked up the battered SUV, and started down the driveway.

A bird called out overhead, and white splattered across the hood of the SUV, missing the dash by inches.

"I'm so glad I'm not shotgun right now." Clay chortled. "Sucks to be you."

Twisting in my seat, I shot him a bird so he wouldn't feel left out, but he only laughed louder.

As we picked up speed, Asa's beautiful hair caught the wind and blew into my eyes, his eyes, and possibly Clay's too.

There was so much of it. And it smelled fantastic as it whipped my cheeks until they stung.

"I have a hairband." I reached in my pocket. "I always carry a spare."

Without slowing, Ace turned onto the main road and switched on the emergency blinkers.

"Would you mind?" His eyes were burnt crimson when he glanced over at me. "I can't braid and drive."

None of us wanted to hang around on Olsen's property longer than necessary, but come on.

"I'm only agreeing to this because none of us can see through your hairnado."

And because I really, really wanted to play with it.

But he didn't need to know that last part.

11

The Kellies had an update for us by the time we reached my room, our unofficial office during this trip. It turned out the missing girl who provoked such a violent reaction from her grieving father was fostered. I don't mean it in the human sense. The girl was entrusted to Olsen to raise for a powerful family in exchange for a boon. Her birth parents likely had heirs to spare and worried she would be picked off by her elder siblings in a coup when it came time for the heir apparent to come into their inheritance.

That meant no adoption paperwork, no birth record, no school records.

And, as far as the Kellies could determine, no missing persons report. Of any kind. With any agency.

"It's like she never existed," I muttered at my screen. "Olsen did his job of hiding her too well."

"He also lied about reporting her missing." Asa tucked a lock of hair behind his ear. "Why bring it up when he knew we had the resources to prove he wasn't telling us the truth?"

"Most folks wouldn't hang around to fact-check a story in an enraged troll's living room while he trashed the place." Clay shrugged. "We sure didn't. Maybe it was an act? Sell us a sob story then hit the bricks?"

"Perhaps," Asa conceded, his expression thoughtful beneath his knotted mane of windblown hair.

"You don't have to keep your hair like that." I did my best not to laugh now that I had the full-on view of my handiwork. "We won't think less of you if you go brush out the tangles."

With only one hairband to spare, I had gathered his hair to my side of the car and plaited a single braid. I got most of it, thanks to its length, but a few flyaways had persisted. Those I shoved through loops in the braid to lock them down and keep them out of his eyes. That treatment, paired with high wind, whipped knots that would require a shower, intensive conditioner, and a comb to fix. Maybe a detangler too.

Did they even make detangler for adults?

Hmm.

Maybe that explained why his scent often carried an undertone of juicy green apples.

"I don't mind." He returned to his work then checked his phone. "They're here to tow the SUV."

"Do they need us for that?" I was busy ordering us a late lunch/early dinner online. "I can go down."

"I tossed the keys on the front seat." Clay kept pecking away. "They'll text if there's a problem."

A chime on my phone had me searching through my pockets for it and frowning at the notification.

"Everything okay?" Clay glanced up then. "You don't look happy."

"It's probably nothing." I opened the security app to be sure. "There was movement near the house."

Slowly, so as not to miss anything, I flipped through the various cameras.

"I don't see anything." I switched screens to check for missed calls. "The wards must be holding steady."

"Colby would call if there was an issue." Asa allowed himself a small grin. "She's already proven that."

"Yeah." I forced myself to breathe. "You're right."

The day had been spent on travel, mostly our snail crawl back to the hotel, but it wasn't full dark yet.

A knock on the door brought my head up, but Clay just smiled and said, "Why don't you get that?"

One eyebrow quirking high, I answered the door to find the promised grocery delivery. A whole lot of it. Somewhere was a store without butter, sugar, flour, eggs, milk, or Clay-approved mix-ins. He also bought a muffin tin, a cookie sheet, and two cake pans with several bottles of nonstick spray.

As the nice young man loaded me down with bags, Clay scooched up behind me then nudged me aside.

Asa met me in the kitchenette, accepted the bags, and began putting away the cold items.

When he caught me staring, again, I was forced to play it off by whipping out my phone. "Smile!"

Caught off guard, Asa did not smile but raised his eyebrows in a questioning look that was now captured forever on my phone. His hair lent him a *just rolled out of bed* appearance while his expression threw off *I haven't had my coffee yet* vibes.

Before he questioned my motives, I spun and snapped a quick pic of Clay loaded down with bags.

"I'm going to send Colby these pics of my two baking assistants."

I did it too, to cover my butt, which wouldn't have been an issue if Asa hadn't looked so adorable.

Yep.

This was definitely his fault. Or his hair's fault. One or the other. Both?

While I helped Clay put away his perishables, Asa returned to the table to resume his work.

There was really only room for one, but two could squish in there thanks to the open floorplan.

"We have preliminary results on the remains found at the processor." Asa scrolled through the email. "They have been positively identified as the fourth missing girl."

"Dammit." A carton of eggs exploded in Clay's fist. "What kind of sicko dreams up something like that?"

"We met a lady who bakes people cookies earlier," I reminded him. "Black Hat exists for a reason."

Look at me, spouting rhetoric I had been force-fed most of my life in the hopes I would one day believe it.

Asa studied me. "Do you think we'll be paying the Malones a visit in the future?"

"If not us, then someone." Of that I had no doubt. "Rose's powers are on lockdown for a reason."

"File a mental note," Clay warned, "and then forget it."

Black Hat had a zero tolerance for cowboying. Rogue agents got dead. It was how a lot of old-timers who wanted out but couldn't quit made their grand exits. They chose their own targets, picked them off, then waited for the kill squad to arrive. That was the worst. No one wanted to terminate a contract.

And yes, that was how the director classified the sanctioned murder of one of his agents.

A contract.

Was it any wonder I had wanted out bad enough to risk a kill squad on my doorstep?

Except that wasn't what happened, and I must have been banking on it. I was too valuable to terminate. Or I had been. Maybe I thought going white witch would turn the Bureau off me. If so, I had been wrong.

Otherwise, I wouldn't be standing here, debating what sweet treat I craved the most.

"I'll bake." I was relieved to work out some of my aggression in the kitchen. "You guys keep working."

By the time dessert was done, the food ought to be here. The cookies I had in mind could cool while we ate dinner.

"Do we get to pick the recipe?" Clay fluttered his lashes at me. "I was thinking..."

"Kitchen sink cookies." I rolled my eyes. "I know what you were thinking. I saw all the ingredients."

While I indulged in my favorite form of relaxation, I attempted to draw our clues into a cohesive whole.

A text from Colby came through while I had sticky fingers, but the preview was laughing emojis.

That brief contact with her lightened my mood enough I could enjoy the simple act of baking.

The sweet and spicy aroma of extra saucy fried chicken wings overpowered my cookies, and I turned to find Clay bringing in the takeout.

Lost in thoughts and memories, I hadn't heard the doorbell or his trek across the room.

"Are you all right?" Asa crowded me to reach the plates in the cabinet. "You're pale."

Details of the Stag case did that to me. When I gave them headspace, they left me cold and empty.

A thirst for power, a hunger for violence. A trail of bodies. His legacy of death might have been mine.

In many ways, it was, or had been. He never shook free of his addictions. I took my sobriety day by day.

"I don't like that there are two previous sets of four missing girls, but we have this random missing girl in the mix. I don't like that a guy who fits our profile has a missing daughter who's not, to our knowledge, one of the victims." I took the last pan of cookies from the oven and turned it off. "I don't like it at all."

"You want to go back out there tomorrow?" Clay accepted the plates from Asa. "It's on the way."

Empty hands freed up Asa to snag three hotel-branded water bottles for us to wash down the food.

Clay had treats on the brain instead of our usual travel staples, so we had to make do or drink milk.

"Yeah." I followed them to the table and cleared space for us to eat. "I want a crack at him."

I couldn't put my finger on what bugged me, but I was rusty in the logical-deduction department. The whopper of a lie he told was more than enough to warrant a return visit, so we could use it as a platform for questioning him further.

We loaded our plates, fought over the cups of ranch dressing, then settled in to eat and take a break.

"Trust your instincts." Asa moved the food around on his plate. "As Clay said, it won't cost us anything."

"This time, let's park farther down the road." I held my sticky fingers up to Asa. "I forgot the napkins."

"I'll get them." He took the hint like a champ. "Need anything else?"

"Nope." I smiled, polite as you please. "That's it."

When he turned his back, I held a finger to my lips where Clay would see, then I switched plates with Asa.

I had been careful not to eat any of mine. I just handled a couple to get saucy fingers. Then I settled in to observe Asa's reaction. I expected him to figure it out before he sat, thanks to Clay's glower, but Asa had napkins in hand, which he passed to me, then sat. I tried very hard not to stare, but I was curious as a cat when it came to him.

"Thanks." I lifted a wing and took a bite. "These honey mustard ones are good."

"I prefer the tongue torcher supreme." Clay sniffled. "You know it's good when your eyes water."

"What about you?" I was totally rocking the covert vibe. "How do you like yours, Asa?"

A frown knit his brow as he brought a wing to his mouth. No. Not his mouth. His nose.

His eyes closed as he inhaled, and when he opened them, they were burnt crimson and fixed on me.

Until this exact moment, I can't say I thought a man eating could get me hot and bothered, but Asa did it without breaking a sweat.

Probably it was how he held my gaze the whole time...then licked his fingers.

"Here." Clay pressed a bottle of icy water into my hand. "You look flushed."

Breaking the staring contest, I smiled weakly at him. "I must have gotten a tongue torcher by mistake."

"That must be it," he said dryly. "I warned you about playing with fire."

"You did." I drank long and deep, drawn right back to Asa's dark stare. "I think I just got burned."

Too bad I got the feeling I wouldn't learn a single thing from the experience.

We had ourselves a conundrum guaranteed to keep me running *what-if* scenarios until my brain gave up and shut off out of sheer exhaustion. It could only spin in so many circles before I got dizzy and fell down.

The Kellies informed us, after our cookies, that Mr. Olsen hadn't been to work in four weeks.

His bosses didn't know anything about a daughter, missing or not, and claimed he was on leave.

But, during that period, three grievances had been filed against him for aggression toward coworkers.

Meaning he had, for whatever reason, shown up to work while he was cleared for an extended vacation.

Those were the only black marks on his record with the company in over twenty years of employment.

Everyone grieved in their own way. I took no issue with Mr. Olsen snapping at people while he mourned.

Could even be that grief drove him to work to occupy his time. If so, why not report in and get paid?

Based on my glimpse of his living situation, he could use the money, so what had kept him coming back to work without compensation? Surely not the goodness of his heart. No one nine-to-fived for that.

A timer buzzed to let me know Colby would be expecting my call in five. After I raked my fingers through my hair, I did my best not to appear sleep deprived or stressed over the case as I dialed her number.

"You remembered." Her face filled the screen. "I feel so special."

"Smarty-pants."

"I don't wear pants."

"Smarty fuzz butt."

"Hey, now that's rude. Do I talk about your butt fuzz?"

Heat crept up my nape when it occurred to me the guys could probably hear every word.

With that in mind, I quickly redirected our conversation. "How are things on the home front?"

"I don't want you to freak out or anything if I tell you this." She eyed me. "Promise?"

"I'm already freaking out hearing those words, so rip off the Band-Aid."

"I miss you." She held up two hands. "Not enough for you to come home or anything."

"Aww." I made kissy noises at her. "I miss you too."

"Eww." She blocked the camera with a wing. "Stop it, or I'll puke."

"Fine." I waited to see her face again. "It's weird hanging out with boys all day."

"Clay seems cool." She cut her eyes toward her computer screen and the battle raging there. "Asa is..."

"...also surprisingly cool." I kept my assessment rated PG. "I haven't worked with a daemon or a fae. He's a twofer. Both halves seem equally cool." I opened my mouth to say more but what came out was, "He's got pretty hair." *Dang it, brain. You had one job.* "Then again, so does Clay. Though I must confess not all wigs are created equal."

"Mmm-hmm."

"Enough about me." I squinted at the screen. "What are you doing?"

"Nothing much right now. Most of my team is asleep."

"This is way early for you guys." I noticed the pile of snacks beside her keyboard. "You stayed up all night." I clutched my chest in feigned shock. "That's why you've got crust in your eyes, and your friends are MIA."

"I don't have crusty eyes." She rubbed at them. "I couldn't sleep anyway."

"I'll give you a one-time pass." I got serious. "It's unnerving any time the wards blink."

Voice small, she asked, "It scares you too?"

"I got lucky my old boss sent Clay after me." I didn't want to get into the details, but Colby was smart. "It could have gotten ugly otherwise." I hesitated. "We're safer with me working for the Bureau again, but...we'll always have to be careful."

"Because you made a lot of powerful enemies."

"Yes."

"And because I'm special."

"Yes."

"I don't mind being a moth," she said after a moment. "Flying is awesome."

A bolt of regret struck me right in the heart, cracking it open for her to see. "I'm glad."

"It will be even cooler once you let me actually be your familiar."

"Um..."

"You're back at work, which means you need a partner." She thumbed her chest. "That's me."

"I have Clay and Asa."

"They're partners, though. You don't have one. You're a third wheel. I would balance the team."

"You make a compelling argument." Smart kids, man. "Let me get through this first assignment, okay?"

Hell would freeze over, thaw out, then freeze again before I let her work this particular case.

"That's not a no, so deal."

"Why do I feel like I was just played?"

A weird chime noise plus a cat yowl poured from her monitor. "Hey, the guys are awake."

"I'm guessing that means you need to go."

"I really need this golden Anubis statue, and Jane promised to help me steal one."

"Have fun storming the castle." I blew her a kiss. "Call if you have trouble sleeping, okay?"

A furry hand blew me a kiss in return. "I will."

I ended the call knowing Colby would be up until dawn and not minding one bit if she bent the rules. The last thing I wanted was for her to be lonely and paranoid while I was too far away to comfort her. Moths were nocturnal, anyway. That's why she had a generous bedtime for her age in the first place. Better she played all night and slept all day while I was traveling than hide in her bedroom, jumping at every noise.

Holding on to the warm glow that came from talking to Colby, I attempted to fall asleep on a high note.

Ten minutes later, I gave up, rolled out of bed, and padded into the kitchen to peek in the fridge.

A carton of blueberries and a produce bag with two lemons caught my eye.

Hmm.

Guess it was going to be a blueberry scone with lemon glaze kind of morning.

12

"I would ask how you slept last night, but I can smell the answer." Clay entered the suite. "Blueberries?"

"Blueberry scones with lemon icing," I confirmed. "I misread the recipe and ended up with three dozen."

One of the many dangers of midnight baking, though no one ever complained about the extras.

"That's guaranteed to be the best news I hear today." He kissed my cheek then shoved me. "Go sit."

The gleam of the overhead lights off his scalp raised my eyebrows. It wasn't often he went au naturel.

"Only because you asked so nicely." I slogged to the table. "I couldn't turn my brain off last night."

A dozen scones stacked on a plate landed in front of me before Clay returned to the kitchen for milk.

His big hands juggled three full glasses with ease, and he set them at our places. "Did you talk to Colby?"

"I did." I smiled goofily. "She told me she misses me."

"I know how she feels." He plopped down across from me. "You leave a big hole when you're gone."

"Black holes are like that," I said sagely. "Sucking everything into them and leaving nothing behind."

"That's not what I meant, and you know it." He kicked me beneath the table. "I hope it won't be another decade until I see you after this." He bit into his first scone and moaned. "Please never leave me again."

It hurt to make him no promises, but I was wary of my good fortune, and it hadn't slipped my notice that the director had yet to contact me. It left me uneasy. I couldn't think of a reason for his silence, and that bothered me.

Unless he was hoping to trick me into believing this time, living under his auspices would be different.

Hey, I might have been born at night, but not last night.

As I washed down my second scone, I couldn't help noticing the empty chair. "Where's Asa?"

"Brushing his hair." Clay snickered into his glass of milk and almost shot it out through his nose. "You did a number on him, Dollface. I told him not to sleep on it, but he fell asleep texting. I tried to help." He sipped again, this time with a pinky held straight up. "Apparently, I have a heavy hand with a comb, and I don't know how to brush *real* hair that's rooted into a person's actual scalp."

Way to hit Clay right in the feels. Asa would be paying for that comment for a *looong* time.

Which was the only reason I didn't press for details about who Asa might have been texting so late.

Wiping my hands clean, I tried for a neutral tone. "Does he need help?"

"I'm sure he does." Clay narrowed his eyes on me. "And you're not going to give it to him."

Oh, yeah. Clay was pissed about the hair comment. No wonder he had gone bald today.

"The thought never crossed my mind." I checked the time. "We need to get on the road soon."

Grumbling around yet another scone, he asked, "Still antsy about Olsen?"

"Kept me up all night." I shoved my plate aside. "I can't put my finger on why it bothers me so much."

That admission earned me a solid frown. "You didn't get any weird vibes while we were there, right?"

"Not a one." I sipped my milk to wet my throat. "It didn't hit me until I read the Kellies' report."

"Must have triggered something in your subconscious."

"Must have." I couldn't shake the jitters. "It feels like I've got ants in my pants."

Licking his fingers clean, Clay rose and pushed back his chair. "Then let's go, with or without Hairnado."

"Clay," I warned him. "Name-calling is beneath you."

"I'm seven feet and change." He grinned. "Most things are beneath me."

"I'll get my kit." I nudged him toward his room. "You get your partner."

The last thing I did before falling asleep, if memory served, was restock my kit, so it was nothing to strap it on. I already had my wand in my pants pocket. I palmed my badge, ID, and wallet, then I was ready.

Much to my relief, and Clay's obvious disgust, Asa emerged with his hair restored to its former glory. His part was sharp, his braids were neat, and they gleamed, still damp, under the light.

As he walked past, I breathed in the scents of tobacco...and green apple.

Rolling my lips in to keep from commenting, I handed him a paper towel I'd loaded with four scones earlier, before Clay polished off the full three dozen. The man was a bottomless pit.

Asa brought them to his nose and inhaled. "You baked these?"

"I did." I tilted my head, mining for an explanation for the game we played. "How could you tell?"

Perhaps sensing my angle, he took his sweet time in answering. "They smell like you."

"Hmm." I appeared to consider that. "Does it bother you?"

Without breaking eye contact, which I was learning was a big thing with him, he selected a scone and bit it clear in half. The way he savored it gave me workplace-inappropriate chills, and I was drawn to the flex of his throat when he swallowed, which left me questioning my sanity.

"No," he rasped when he was done. "It doesn't bother me at all."

"Yeah, well, *this* bothers me." Clay pointed at Asa and then at me. "Whatever *this* is, stop it."

Asa didn't look away from me when he said, "It's too late for that."

"Um." I faced a sudden need to swallow, dare I say gulp. "Explain *too late* for me?"

Neither one enlightened me, which made me want to hex them with warts on their unmentionables.

Goddess bless, this was sad. Warts? Really? I truly had lost my touch.

We gathered our equipment, loaded into the SUV, and set out for a visit to Mr. Olsen.

Without Asa causing inconvenient flutters in my stomach, I had room for dread to spread its wings.

The front door hadn't been repaired or replaced. That was our first hint Mr. Olsen had flown the coop.

The moment we learned he lied about filing a missing persons report, we should have doubled back.

Final confirmation from the Kellies hit my inbox around five this morning, but we waited until sunrise.

The holdout had been the troll-ruling body itself, the agency a troll in a tricky situation, like a foster gone missing, would most likely approach for help. The clerics had to be convinced to share information regarding a foster with outsiders through a donation to their order. Eventually, they verified the girl existed, and who was responsible for her, but they hadn't been made aware she had gone missing.

We had kicked a hornets' nest in bringing the situation to their attention. I wasn't sorry it would be passed upline to the director. I was only sorry the director wasn't allergic to hornet stings.

Ever the optimist, Clay offered, "Maybe Olsen stayed in a hotel last night?"

"Maybe," I allowed for Clay's sake. "Let's take him up on his open-door invitation."

"There is no door," Asa said wryly. "Are you sure we ought to intrude?"

"Yes." I exited the vehicle, before he tried his hand at changing my mind, and went still. "Oh crap."

The smell hit me and woke that dark part lurking on the periphery of my self-control.

"We've got bodies." I had no doubt they smelled it too. "Black magic?"

Asa and Clay exited the SUV and flanked me while I read the area from a safe distance.

"Yes," Asa confirms. "It's quite ripe."

As much as I wanted to cringe from a descriptor that might apply to me too, I forced my shoulders back. I was who I was, and there was no changing that. His opinion of me couldn't matter. Not now. Not here.

Drawing my wand, I approached the rusting travel trailer, the stench more potent as we neared it.

"Whatever is in there has been there for a while." I was betting four weeks. "How did Olsen hide this?"

"A circle?" Clay stuck close. "That's all I can figure."

Wards allowed air to pass over and through them. Circles could go either way. Breathable or airtight.

"Unless what we're about to discover," Asa added his two cents, "wasn't put there until after we left."

Just like old times, I went in first. Unlike old times, they allowed it because the property was vacant.

The lack of heartbeats told me what their keen noses and other senses had already relayed to them.

Black magic might not register to my nose, but the sweet-and-sour tang of rot hit me hard.

I followed it into the back bedroom and found what I expected to see. A dead troll well into decomp. His killer, and it was male, had driven a railroad spike through his heart. The rust told me it was old and iron.

Trolls were fae, and cold iron was a death sentence.

I could only hope he was dead before the killer sliced off his face with surgical precision.

"This must be the real Mr. Olsen." I squatted next to him, examining his body for clues. "Why kill him?"

"I think I can answer that." Asa waited several feet behind me. "Look."

Standing, I trailed Clay into a tiny room beside the master. "The missing daughter."

The door to her bedroom wasn't substantial, but it had been kicked open, meaning she locked herself in.

"That's a House Thorn dagger in her chest." Asa made a gesture of prayer. "She committed suicide."

"Seppuku?" I backed from the room once confirming his assessment. "A ritual suicide."

"Similar," he agreed, then glanced back at Mr. Olsen. "The girl must have been targeted through her father." He exhaled slowly. "The copycat came for her, here, and she misread his intent."

"She thought her family came for her." I shut my eyes. "She took her life rather than let them kill her."

"Mr. Olsen must have heard the commotion from the yard," Clay theorized, "or maybe he just got home from work. He came to check on her and got a railroad spike to the chest for his trouble."

"That narrative fits what we're seeing." I left the bodies to search the rest of the trailer. "We'll know for sure after the lab tells us time of death." I thought back on the timeline. "Four weeks." I rubbed my nape as the full implications hit me. "This might have been the copycat's first victim. Make that *victims*."

The director really had wasted no time coming to find me as soon as he required my specific skill set.

"He could have glamoured himself to resemble Olsen and used his identity to stalk the other victims and their kill sites." Asa picked up my train of thought. "That would explain the complaints against him."

"He took Olsen's face." A technique I hadn't seen used in ages. "Literally."

"A masque?" Asa glanced back at Olsen. "That's old magic."

Glamour accomplished the same thing, really, and it was easier to cast and dispel. More versatile too.

A masque was exactly what you would think. A mask of dried skin, a face, that you wore over your own. It drew the power to transform you into that person, and only that person, from the target's own death.

"The killer must have been well and truly pissed at Olsen to expend that much magic on a trinket."

Masques had limited use, given each was only good for one face, but that had never been the point.

Their creation was rooted in punishment rather than practicality.

"The killer moves on the girl. The girl robs him of his prize." Clay mulled it over. "Olsen hears her scream and comes running. The killer murders Olsen in a fit of rage."

"The killer assumes Olsen's identity, but he doesn't know Olsen is on vacation." Asa continued his search for more evidence. "He didn't plan for this. His first kills, and he's already made two mistakes." He gazed across the space. "Maybe he decides he's found an ideal scapegoat to pin his crimes on when he's done. He makes the best of it by setting up shop at Olsen's place, and that's when he makes the masque."

"If we're even half right, we've flushed out the killer." That was the good news. The bad news was, "That means he'll be on the move."

Harder to corner prey when it knows it's being hunted and by whom. The killer's acting skills tricked Clay *and* Asa into believing him. No doubt, he would have fooled me too. He had channeled the rage over his discovery into an authentic facsimile of grief. He hurled accusations at them about how no one cared his daughter was missing to keep them off-balance and defensive.

They left, we all did, with a sense of having disturbed a good man, a good *father*, in mourning.

"He slept and ate here." Clay indicated food in the fridge and sheets on the couch. "But that's it."

"The car is gone." Asa pulled out his phone. "I'll issue a BOLO for it and Olsen."

"Keep it on our network," Clay advised. "We don't want humans confronting him."

"That will greatly reduce its efficiency," Asa pointed out. "There are more teams in the area but..."

As predicted, those teams were happy to let Black Hat's black witch take on the rogue black witch solo.

"He's right." I sided with Clay. "We don't want to give him an excuse to further involve humans."

Asa took his calls outside, as if privacy was an issue, but I bet the smell was tweaking his sensitive nose.

"He's going to run to his safe place." Clay surveyed the area one last time. "We find that, we find clues."

"Let's hope we get lucky with the APB." I exited the trailer. "Otherwise, we might lose him."

There were days between the discovery of his victims and his search for new ones. We were in the lull.

"He was already hunting." I filled my lungs with fresh air. "He might have his first victim chosen."

I moseyed over to Asa to see if he had made any progress while Clay reported the crime to the Bureau, which would further complicate the situation between the director and the enraged trolls.

"Are you sure?" Asa paced a tight line. "Yes." He came to sudden halt. "Give me the address."

Ending the call, Asa tapped his phone against his chin. "We have a lead."

"You don't look thrilled about it." I was of the opinion any lead was a good lead. "What's the deal?"

"Olsen owned a tract of land about an hour from here. It's a thirty-acre forested spread."

And that, friends, was where he had invested his money. "His hunting grounds."

A troll could only ape human for so long before instinct demanded he obey his nature.

Plus, they required room to spread out their caches. Thirty acres was plenty for that.

"The copycat couldn't afford to compound the mistakes he already made. He would have performed an inventory on the troll's belongings before committing to that identity. A remote tract of land might have been the tipping point in Olsen's favor." Asa put away his cell. "There's no record of a structure on the property, but I'm sure Olsen had a small cabin, or even a cave, for when he hunted in inclement weather. Trolls don't fare well in the cold."

"This could be it." A wave of nerves and nausea tangled in my gut. "Do we call for backup?"

"He's on alert thanks to our visit." Asa hummed. "We should take our chances before he bolts."

"I'm good with that." I wanted this over and done. I wanted to go home. To Colby. "Let's do it."

"Don't I get a vote?" Clay stomped over to us. "I have opinions too."

"We were waiting on you to make it unanimous." I patted his arm. "Well? What do you think?"

"I agree with Ace," he grumped. "If we don't want to lose him, we have to move."

"All righty then." I got in the SUV, checked my phone, then settled in. "You have the address?"

Asa tapped the side of his head then fed the information to his phone's GPS for the quickest route.

The best of all possible outcomes was the copycat had yet to take his first victim for his next piece.

The churn in my gut warned me not to get my hopes up, but it also reminded me what I had done to the man responsible for inspiring this killer. Nerves weren't all to blame for my upset stomach. Hunger was a yawning void within me that hadn't been filled in too long.

This killer was ruthless, powerful, merciless.

His heart would taste...delicious.

13

The address wasn't hard to find. There was a mailbox and everything. That led me to trust Clay was right about his hunch we would find some form of troll-friendly accommodations on the property. Where, we had no idea. And the farther we trekked, the deeper into the killer's territory we roamed. If he was using this property to hold his victims, he would know the area well. He could be watching us from higher ground right now, which blasted chills down my arms.

Up to this point, I had felt relatively safe with Asa and Clay for backup, given my diminished state.

But hunting this killer in his habitat? Without my mantle of power, I was afraid. For us all.

"We can't afford to waste much more time." Clay broke the silence of the past hour with what we must all be thinking. "Assuming the killer came here after we visited him, he could have taken what he needed and bolted last night."

"We don't know what time he left the trailer," Asa agreed. "He could be long gone by now."

"Okay." I was already outvoted. "Let's call in the other..."

A familiar scent hit my nose as a strong wind kicked up in the trees.

"Diesel." Clay picked it up too. "Do you hear a motor?"

The same fuel the killer used to douse his trail to and from his kill sites.

Birdlike, Asa cocked his head. "A generator."

A predatory smile curved my lips as the hunt sang in my blood, louder and louder, deafening my fears.

The burnt crimson smoldering in Asa's eyes called to me, like to like, and he growled low in his throat.

"I'll lead." Clay was used to playing muscle. "Rue, you're the middle. Ace, you bring up the rear."

From what I had gleaned, Asa might prove the superior tracker, but Clay was unkillable. He could be hurt or put out of commission, but if you knew what you were doing, he always came back. Not that it meant I enjoyed him taking one for the team. I didn't. One peek at Asa told me he wasn't a fan either.

But we all had our roles to play, and Clay's had always been as my shield.

The steady purr of the generator led us to the remains of a cabin nature had done its best to reclaim. An orange power cord stretched from the generator through a broken window, giving us the only indication the decrepit structure was habitable.

We saw no sign of the occupant, who may or may not have given up his masque for his true face, but he had gone through the trouble of leaving a steady noise to provide cover for his movements. It worked as much for us as it did against us. The generator might be a decoy he left running after he spent the night out here.

If that was the case, I doubt he intended to come back. Why waste precious resources otherwise?

"No matter how I look at this," I told the guys softly, "he anticipated a visit from us today."

The crime scenes were too fastidious for me to believe he was careless in any regard.

"Who wants to go in?" Clay didn't wait for an answer, he volunteered himself. "Ace, watch her back."

As the mostly indestructible one, Clay ducked into the cabin and was absorbed by its shadows.

"I don't like this," I murmured. "It feels like my skin wants to crawl off my bones."

I identified it as an amplified version of the sensation that convinced me Olsen was worth a second look.

Black magic might not *smell* rank to me, but maybe I had switched the balance within myself enough for its presence to register as danger in my subconscious. Handy if I could hone it into conscious awareness.

Five minutes passed with no sign of Clay. Asa and I made the wordless decision to investigate. Together.

Using my wand as an atmospheric measuring stick, I tapped it once against a random log then gritted my teeth against the feedback. Negative energy permeated the building from the foundation to the roof. An almost foul breath of air expelled when we reached the threshold, and I braced as a dark figure loomed.

"Don't shoot." Clay held up both his hands. "It's just me."

"No offense." I pricked my finger, murmured a spell, and wiped the blood on his arm. "It's him."

When hunting a killer with a penchant for stealing faces and identities, you can't be too careful.

"The cabin is a front." He ground his molars. "The bedroom is nothing but a set of stairs leading down into a cavern. I'm too big to fit very far, but we've found his home away from home."

"What aren't you telling us?" Asa searched his face. "What did you see?"

"There are newspaper clippings." Clay exhaled. "There are candid photos of Colby too."

"I need to get down there." I didn't ask or wait for permission. "I have to see this."

The climb down was well lit, thanks to the generator powering miles of string lights.

The main cave, which soared twelve feet high, split off into four different rooms. It was obvious this was the troll's true home. A couch and recliner sat on a rug in front of a TV on a stand. The closest room had been converted into a simple kitchen with a fridge and a microwave. From the smell, it was plain another one had been used as a bathroom. But the smallest of them, the one that called to me the loudest, had once been a library. Until someone dumped the books on the sofa and made it a shrine.

Yellowed newspaper clippings from the Silver Stag case were taped to the wall in chronological order.

Layers of brittle tape curled, as if this mural had been taken down and put up many times over the years and the artist didn't want to risk damaging the paper further. The fae presses had the most extensive coverage, but the major para newspapers—all magicked to appear blank to humans—had run the story.

Candids of Clay and me from those days filled spots here and there on the wall, but the bottom row...

For a moment, my heart forgot how to beat, and my blood turned to ice water in my veins.

Those photos were recent, taken within the last few weeks. If I had to date them, I bet I would find they were shot in the time since the first victims were found. The wards kept humans from seeing Colby, but paras could pick her out fine. The killer had taken a keen interest in her based on this spread.

There were dozens of photos of her. Just her. Her face. Her wings. Her legs. The rest of the mural might have been an afterthought compared to his dedicated study of her. Maybe he wanted to consume the one soul to escape the Stag and thus prove his superiority over his idol?

But how? *How* did he know about her? No one knew about Colby. She was my best kept secret.

The only way he could have discovered her existence was if...he was there.

The night she died.

The night I saved her.

The night I damned her.

"I have to go." I stumbled back and fell onto the stairs, unable to pry my gaze from the collage. "Now."

"Come on." Asa helped me stand then guided me up into the cabin. "I've got you."

"I called the Bureau." Clay wrapped an arm around me. "They're sending another team to handle this."

"I'm calling in Malone," Asa announced. "I want his input on this scene versus the previous ones."

Our newest CI, criminal informant, could tie this case up for us with a bow. I just struggled to care.

All I could see was my first good look at Colby. All I could hear was her broken voice begging for my help.

I promised to protect her, keep her safe, and I was failing at the only job I ever had that mattered.

"This was a trap." I blinked to clear my eyes, and tears poured over my cheeks. "She's—"

"Shh." Asa embraced my other side. "Not here."

Forced to keep a wary eye out for the killer, we paced ourselves, causing the trek back to the SUV to take an eternity.

None of us spoke until the SUV's tires hit the main road.

"This was a trap," I repeated my earlier words. "He lured me away from home to clear a path to Colby."

The ward blink and the security notifications took on sinister implications that twisted my stomach.

"Who is this guy?" Clay pounded a fist into his open palm. "Why fixate on the Silver Stag? Why Colby?"

I recognized the attempt to distract me for what it was, but I was happy to embrace it.

"The Stag had no family. No friends." I reached back in my memory for those details. "He was a ghost."

"Not a ghost." Clay grunted. "An outlier. He lived off the grid with minimal social interaction. His victims were taken from big box stores. He moved around a lot so as not to draw attention to himself. He had at least forty-eight kills under his belt before he took the last group. We may never know the grand total."

"We got lucky that Colby was a type one diabetic. She got hypoglycemic at the drop of a hat." How times had changed. She lived on sugar now. "She wore a medical alert bracelet her parents had imbued with a locator spell so that if she had an episode outside the house, they could find her. We followed it right to him. He was in the process of transforming the girls for the hunt. Two of their souls were already outside their bodies, wrapping them in his chosen form. He consumed them while I hammered at his ward."

Rage had consumed me, not over the girls' deaths, those hadn't affected me then, but at my inability to beat him at his own game. No wonder, with all the souls he had devoured over the centuries of his life.

But I had Grandfather's voice ringing in my ears, the phantom agony of his cane striking a lash across my hands for each failure. Fury and hatred had burned through me and incinerated the ward. I smashed through the barrier, stabbed the Stag in the gut with my wand, and cursed him with delight. Then, I did what all black witches do to ensure their rivals don't get a shot at revenge.

I ate his foul, black heart.

"Then you saved Colby," Asa finished the story. "Who else would have known that part?"

"I thought no one saw." I rubbed my arms. "The third girl had been transformed when I broke in, but she spooked when the other girls were consumed. She broke out of the pen and ran." I didn't blame her one bit. "Clay chased after her. The Stag was as good as dead at that point. He used everything he had left to transform Colby into a moth. He couldn't move. She had to fly to him." He gave her wings rather than hooves, so she could sail to her own death. "I finished him off before he touched her, then I had an armful of sobbing moth-girl and some hard choices to make."

"It took two teams three days to find the third girl, but her soul had evaporated beyond saving by then." A thoughtful expression settled across Clay's features. "We assumed the fourth girl, Colby, met the same fate."

"That was the plan." I toyed with my seat belt. "All this time, I thought it worked."

"As far as I was concerned, it did." Clay rubbed his smooth head. "I had no idea."

"I should have told you." I wet my lips. "I should have trusted you." I forced out the rest, because I didn't want him getting ideas about me being good for goodness' sake. "I think...I was afraid if I told you what I had done, and I caved to temptation, you would never look at me the same way again."

"If you had told me," he said quietly, "I would have helped in any way I could, to whatever end."

To whatever end.

"I know that now." I blinked to keep tears from sliding down my cheeks. "I couldn't see it then."

Clamping a hand on my shoulder, Clay squeezed. "Are you booking our flight, or do I get the honors?"

"You do it." I folded my hands in my lap. "I'm so jittery I might book us a rocket to the moon."

The seat groaned when Clay leaned back, and his soft voice soothed as he used voice commands to walk his phone through purchasing our tickets.

Asa stole a glance at me. "Will you call Colby to warn her?"

"I tried." I held my phone in a death grip. "She didn't answer."

The flight home from Charlotte was an hour and forty-five minutes.

Four hours had lapsed between the moment we left Olsen's property until we hit the city limits.

Colby still wasn't answering her phone or returning texts, and the security cameras had all gone dark.

I was ready to scream. Or punch something. Or scream while I punched something.

The drive home from the airport took forever, and I didn't wait for Asa to stop before I jumped out. I ran to the gate, casting my senses wide for the wards that had protected us for so long. They were dormant.

The copycat had beaten us here, and he had bypassed my security when he couldn't outright destroy it.

That familiar rage boiled in my gut over a fellow practitioner getting one over on me, but this time it was the result of terror, not a matter of pride.

After flinging open the gate, I jogged up the steps onto the front porch. The first step told me the ward on the house itself had been cracked open. There were no signs of forced entry, but the doorknob turned in my hand without resistance. The silence of a dark and empty house greeted me.

Colby's name burned down my throat, eager to escape, but I didn't want to lure her out until we cleared the house. Room by room, I checked every nook and cranny, using a minor spell to sense her.

"She's not here." I swallowed the panic in my voice. "But that's okay."

"You mentioned she had safe places." Asa touched my elbow. "Let's check those."

"The house is clear," Clay confirmed. "The wards are down, the power's out, and my cell has no signal."

The killer must have laid hexes on the wards when he dropped them, forming a dead zone within their boundaries.

"That gives us a timeframe. He was here six or seven hours ago." I checked my messages. "That's the last time I heard from Colby."

"He's come and gone." Asa rubbed his thumb over my arm. "But he might be hunting her."

"Let's do a circuit of the property," Clay suggested. "Once we clear it as best we can, we'll fetch Colby."

Certainty rang through his voice that she would be safe and sound, and I clung to that by my fingernails.

"Okay." I led them out the back door. "We can start on the north corner and work our way in."

Within seconds, Asa had given himself over to his daemon, whose eyes burned with determination.

"Smell better," he said by way of explanation. "Stronger too."

A nod was all I could spare him as I hit the tree line and began walking the fence that enclosed my land. I couldn't shake the sensation of being watched, but that came from knowing the witch we hunted was gifted in the art of concealment. If we weren't careful, we could lead him straight to Colby.

When we reached the point where we began, Clay slanted his eyes toward me. "Satisfied?"

"Not even close." I offered him a weak smile. "Let's check her cubbies."

The first four yielded nothing but a flash of renewed hope. Each one was secured by a functional spell.

That meant the most critical of all my wards had held and that Colby, if she'd reached a cubby, was safe.

Around the ninth location, I began to sweat, and the twelfth left me with shaking hands.

Before I unwound the spell on lucky thirteen, I shut my eyes and sent up a prayer to anyone listening.

As soon as the magic winked out, a small white blur rocketed out in a frenzy of fuzz and wings.

Next thing I knew, a cat-sized moth smacked me in the face. Her legs wrapped around my head in a death grip, and I got a mouthful of furry abdomen. Wings beat against my ears, deafening me, but I didn't care one whit.

"Rue," she sobbed onto the top of my head. "I was so scared."

"I know." I tugged her down until I could see again and cradled her against my chest. "Me too."

"He walked right in." She clung to me. "It was like the wards weren't even there."

"You didn't see him before he walked through the gate?"

"I was online." Her feathery antennae quivered. "The power cut out, and I went to check the breakers."

Our house was old, and her rig had shorted out her room more than once when she got plug happy.

"That's when I saw him." Her feet bit into me. "He was dressed like Clay and Asa."

Clay had come up behind us, and his lips thinned to a hard line. "*Just* like us or a little different?"

"Just like you." Colby peeked up at him. "I worried something had happened, that he was coming to tell me Rue was hurt." She sniffed. "I tried to call, but my cell wouldn't work, and the landline was down."

Yet another country living necessity—the nearly extinct residential landline phone.

"He must have hoped if he couldn't get through the wards, she would let him in." Asa had shifted back while I had my hands full. "He isolated her to incite panic, to scare her into cooperating."

Smart as Colby was, she was still a kid. She might have done just that if he preyed on her emotions.

"Let's get back to the house." I kissed the top of her head. "I don't like us being out in the open."

Clay and Asa cleared the house to ensure no one had sneaked in while we were away. I raised the wards again, for all the good it would do us, and Clay got the power back on. Colby stuck to me like glue, and it didn't bother me one bit. Neither did Asa's presence at my back, watching over us both.

Once we got things as close to normal as we could manage, I parked Colby at her rig and encouraged her to plug in so we could discuss the Kellies' report on the cave without upsetting her further. Clay and Asa laid out our usual setup on the kitchen table, but I kept my chair pulled back far enough I could see Colby in the next room.

More importantly, she could see me.

Not many kids would be happy for a former black witch to play guardian angel, but she wasn't most kids.

"Our copycat was definitely keeping the girls in the cave." Clay read the first page. "That smell? It wasn't a bathroom. That's not how Olsen used it, anyway. That room was chockful of canned goods and bottled water. A bit of a prepper's paradise." He wiped a hand over his mouth. "There was an anteroom between two shelves we missed because it wasn't lit. The killer installed a barred security door to lock the girls in there."

That far out in the woods, and that deep in the ground, no one would have heard their screams.

"No fingerprints on the mural, despite the tape," Asa added, "but those are easily wiped with magic."

"The generator was dead when they arrived." I rubbed my jaw. "It had a twenty-four-hour fuel tank."

"What bothers me isn't that timeline," Asa said, "but the one here."

"We know the killer was in Samford—" Clay checked his watch, "—nine hours ago now."

"There have been multiple incidents, minor ones, since you left." Asa tapped a finger on the table. "All of them easily explained away."

A shiver of dread rippled down my spine. "Are you saying we've got a *pair* of copycats?"

"That's a big leap," Clay warned. "The evidence doesn't support your theory."

"One killer at the trailer, selecting victims," Asa suggested. "The other in the cave, keeping them alive."

"You think one killer stayed in North Carolina after I arrived," I murmured, "and the other came here."

From the first night, the second killer had been nosing around the property, testing its defenses.

Yes.

That felt right.

"It's a compelling argument," Clay allowed. "For now, let's track the killer we know."

That was the whole problem. We didn't know him. Potentially either of them. Not yet.

An idea tickled the back of my mind. "Do we have the recordings of the first two crime scenes?"

"The Kellies sent them over with the third you requested," Asa confirmed. "I'll email you both a link."

"Here we go," I murmured, clicked, and then swore. "The same person filmed this."

The style was the same, and *style* wasn't a word I ever heard used in reference to crime scene footage.

"Billy Kidd," Asa supplied when I blanked. "I'll check the second recording for credits."

Less than a minute later, he came back with confirmation the same agent had done all the camera work.

"The Bureau called in multiple teams." Clay watched his screen, a deep line bisecting his wide brow. "It's not surprising one guy, let alone a junior agent, got stuck with the drudgework."

Grasping at straws, I was grasping at straws, and I didn't care. We had no other leads. We had nothing.

"Get the Kellies to draw us a timeline of Billy Kidd's movements the last few days." We could start there. "If they push back, tell them we have an eyewitness account. Our suspect is, or might be impersonating, a Black Hat agent." I had another idea. "Can you pull up a photo of Agent Kidd?" I flipped through my files and hit pay dirt. "I've got one of Olsen."

In seconds, Asa emailed me the image, and I carried my laptop to where Colby sat in her rig.

"Hey, punk." I tested a theory. "Can you look at a couple of pictures for me?"

The quick swivel of her eyes toward me confirmed she had been listening in and not playing her game.

Given what she had been through, I didn't have it in me to scold her for disobeying me.

"Yeah." She removed the headset. "What kind of pictures?"

"Nothing bad," I rushed to assure her. "I have two headshots of possible suspects."

"Okay." She studied my screen when I pivoted it toward her. "I don't recognize either of them."

I didn't ask her if she was sure. I didn't want to pressure her into making a false ID to please me.

"Thanks." I lifted her headset. "Try turning this on next time."

Her antennae drooped at having been caught, but she didn't apologize, and I doubt she obeyed me.

Kids these days.

This was why I wasn't cut out to be a mother. I could do the auntie deal, but parenting was too hard.

Back at the table, I joined the others and shook my head, though I was sure they overheard us.

"She cleared Olsen and Kidd." I hadn't meant to say it out loud, but disappointment pushed it out of me. "That doesn't mean much, as far as Olsen is concerned. We don't know who took over his identity." That brought me to another salient point. "And, if there are two of them, they might both be wearing masques."

Humans had it so much easier. Their criminals' disguises were laughable in comparison to the magic that allowed skilled practitioners, in multitudes of disciplines, to fundamentally change their appearance on a whim. Some paranormal creatures, like fae, were even born with the skill as camouflage to protect them from human detection.

But it also made it twice as hard to pin a crime on them without DNA evidence left at the scene.

"The Kellies checked in." Clay had his phone in hand, but his gaze swung to mine. "Kidd is MIA."

A tiny flame of hope kindled in my chest. "How long?"

"He hasn't been back to work since the day we examined the third crime scene."

"Okay." I itched to jump up and pace. "Now we're getting somewhere."

"They're going to check flight manifests and car rental services, see if they can pin down his movements. It says here they checked his hotel. His room was empty. There were no signs of foul play. He appears to have left of his own free will." Clay frowned. "They're sending a unit to his house in Oregon for a welfare check."

"What about his partner?" I couldn't recall his name. "Does he know why Kidd bolted?"

"Their hotel was booked solid. A fishing tournament." Clay shook his head. "They had separate rooms on different floors. Both singles. No suites available. The senior agent went to check on Kidd when he failed to show at the car."

"And found the room empty," I finished for him. "Are there security cameras at the hotel?"

Kidd was a warg. He couldn't cloak himself and walk out unnoticed. He would be visible.

"There are," Clay confirmed. "They all went dark for twenty minutes around midnight the night before."

Tech could have done that. Magic could have done it faster and easier. But wargs didn't have magic.

Proof we had two killers working together? Or evidence our cinematographer was also a hacker?

"We need to contact the Bureau," I decided. "Let them know he's a person of interest in our case."

But if there were two of them...and they had been coordinating with one another...

"Get the Kellies to cross-check the agents present at each scene." I let my attention drift back to the film. "We know Kidd was there, so the senior agent assigned to him was too. Who else?"

"You won't want to hear this, but you need to rest." Clay checked the time. "It's almost eleven."

The whole day was a blur of frantic movement and panicked thoughts, but I couldn't stop yet.

"Colby is exhausted." Asa hit me where it hurt. "I guarantee she won't sleep a wink without you."

Poor thing was in her rig, but she was drooping. Her antennae hung in her eyes, but she didn't care.

"I'll work through the night." Clay made it a promise. "If I get anything good, I'll wake you."

"Okay." I raised my hands in defeat. "I'll sit with her long enough to put her to sleep."

Leaving the guys to continue digging, I edged toward Colby, who was deathly pale for a white moth.

"I don't want to sleep." She kept staring at the screen, but it was obvious she wasn't seeing it. "I'm fine."

"You're not fine. I'm not fine. No one is fine." I removed her headset and scooped her into my arms. "It's been a rough day for all of us." I aimed us down the hall. "Let's curl up in your room and unwind."

"Okay." She snuggled closer. "We can do that."

The door to her bedroom stood ajar, and I nudged it wider with my foot.

We discovered along the way that she slept best in a more natural environment. I papered the walls in a forest mural, painted the ceiling with blue skies—thankfully a sea sponge did most of the work for me—and matched it with green carpet. She opted to ditch her bed, and instead, I had filled the space with tall artificial plants I fastened to the floor to support her weight if she decided to light on them. In the center of it all, I had strung a Colby-sized hammock that blended with her surroundings. I set her down in there.

In the far corner, a gray beanbag chair, representative of a rock, gave me a place to lounge with her.

"I'm going to veg on my phone," I told her. "You shut your eyeballs."

"I can't shut my eyeballs, but I can close my eye*lids*."

"Don't sass your elders, smarty fuzz butt." I switched off the light with an effort of will. "Sweet dreams."

14

A tickle along the edge of my senses roused me around five in the morning, and I eased off the beanbag to investigate. Immediately, I regretted my life choices. Pretty sure my back snapped in half while I slept.

Colby was out like a light, so I tiptoed from the room, leaving the door open a crack.

The kitchen glowed warm and welcoming in the otherwise dark house, and I headed there.

"Hey, sleepyhead." Clay glanced up from his screen and rubbed his dry eyes. "Everything okay?"

A notable absence in the room caused me to reconsider my answer. "Where's Asa?"

"Doing a perimeter check." He stretched his arms over his head. "He's been out there maybe five minutes."

"Ah." I joined him at the table. "I sensed a disturbance through the wards."

"Sorry about that." Clay swept his gaze over me. "I didn't realize you were that sensitive."

"Paranoia," I said by way of explanation, and he grunted under-standing. "Any updates?"

"We heard from Malone." He leaned back in his chair. "He said the fuel used in the generator is a match for what he smells at the kill sites. An exact match. As in, Olsen must have hoarded fuel too."

There was no telling what the Bureau would turn up when all was said and done. There would be caches all over that property. And who better to ferret them out than an ornery lynx with a nose for the killer?

"Ask Malone if he would be willing to help the teams locate the various caches."

"I'm sure he'll be happy to help," Clay said dryly. "You give great motivational speeches."

Intimidating little old ladies, even ones who baked people cook-ies, wasn't a talent I wanted to cultivate.

More emails of lesser importance arrived, requiring my atten-tion, and I settled in with Clay to work.

Two hours later, deep in research, I almost jumped out of my skin when a hand landed on my shoulder.

"I didn't mean to startle you." Asa raised said hand like he had been burned. "I was just reporting in."

Blinking away the lines of text behind my eyes, I stared up at him. "Find anything?"

"Nothing." The edges of his lips twitched. "Except for an elderly woman with a yellow camo shotgun."

"She's up with the dawn." I stood in a rush. "How long ago did you see her?"

My neighbors didn't expect me home yet, and I had left my car in the driveway. That meant they had no way to gauge my return unless they saw me with their own eyes. The sight of a strange SUV in my yard must have sent Mrs. Gleason into a tizzy. Enough she walked our property line for a read on who had dared to trespass while I was away.

"She's been on high alert since Clay dropped in unannounced." I didn't have to remind Clay she pumped his butt full of buckshot. "She might have seen or heard something we can use. I'll go talk to her."

"Not alone, you won't." Clay made it an order. "Ace, you go with her."

Asa cocked an eyebrow in response, clearly not expecting to be paired with me.

"The kid likes me better," Clay said smugly. "She's less likely to panic if she wakes up alone, and I'm here."

"Fair point." Asa lowered his head. "All right."

"Let's take my ride." I touched his arm. "That way, she probably won't shoot when she sees us."

"Probably?" Asa flicked a glance at me. "I thought you were friends."

"We are." I shrugged. "But she's got arthritis, and that makes for a twitchy trigger finger."

Before we left, I changed into a casual outfit to further put Mrs. Gleason at ease.

Asa didn't take his eyes off me, or the knee-length sundress with bumblebees zooming across the fabric.

There was no time to start a conversation worth having in under two minutes, so the drive was silent.

Sure enough, I pulled in, and Mrs. Gleason stepped out onto her porch with the gun in her hands.

Careful not to make any sudden movements, I lowered my window and called out, "Good morning."

"Rue?" She eased down the stairs, the shotgun tucked under her arm. "I wasn't expecting you back yet." She spotted Asa halfway to me and froze. "You brought a friend." She glared at him. "Are you that police looking into Rue's ex?"

After he got his window down, he answered, "Yes, ma'am."

"Good." She came to my side. "Another police was by your place yesterday. Around five. He was dressed like this one, anyway. Not as pretty, though." She gave Asa a more thorough examination. "I figured he was checking on your house while you were gone, so I didn't shoot him."

Smothering the urge to laugh, I cleared my throat. "I appreciate that."

Tone polite, Asa coaxed her. "Can you describe him for us?"

"About the height of my late husband. Maybe five-eight or five-nine. Brown hair. Nice suit."

On my phone, I accessed the photos of Olsen and Kidd. "Did you see either of these men?"

"No." She shook her head. "That wasn't him."

So much for that idea. Illusion magic truly was a plague on the paranormal law enforcement community.

"I don't understand." She frowned. "If he's a police, then can't you call the station for that information?"

"We're concerned my ex—" I lied through my teeth, "—might be impersonating a police officer to evade capture." I poured it on thick. "We have reason to believe he discovered my new address." I put a cherry on top. "I think he might be who you saw at my house."

"I knew I should have shot him," she growled. "That's the last time I give the benefit of the doubt."

This visit was quickly spinning out of my control. "I would prefer you not go around shooting people."

"On your property, that's your choice." She patted her shotgun. "On mine, I believe in instant karma."

As soon as this was handled, I owed her granddaughter a call. She had to talk Mrs. Gleason down for me.

"We appreciate your time." I squeezed her hand. "Do me a favor?"

"I already said I wouldn't shoot anyone on your property," she grumbled. "What else do you need?"

"If you see him again—or anyone else—call my cell. Do *not* go after him. He's armed and dangerous."

"Well, what do you know?" Her smile was feline. "So am I."

"Please?" I squeezed her hand. "I couldn't bear it if something happened to you because of me."

"All right." She leaned in to kiss my cheek then stepped away. "I'll call a meeting of the Yard Birds."

"Thank you." I raised my window and backed onto the main road. "Well, that got us nowhere."

Asa didn't agree or disagree. "Who are the Yard Birds?"

"They're our neighbors, and a few of her friends. They're our unofficial neighborhood watch."

That made him smile. "Are you sure it's wise to let her rally her troops?"

"We don't have much choice." I rolled into my driveway. "It's probably a good thing. They'll keep her too busy to get into trouble." I parked with a sigh. "They meet every Sunday after church. The last time, they drank their weight in margaritas and ended up passed out on the porch and in the driveway."

Genuine alarm sharpened his expression. "With guns?"

"One of them is always chosen to be the designated ammo holder. So, yes to guns. No to bullets."

"You have interesting neighbors," he mused. "Are you sure they'll be okay unsupervised?"

"I have the numbers of their husbands and grandkids if they get too out of hand."

Back home, we exited the vehicle in time to find a moth on the porch, judging us.

Behind her, standing guard, was Clay. He rubbed the smile off his face at our cold reception.

"You left." Colby landed on my head and knocked on my skull with a hand. "Why would you do that?"

"We have to find this guy." I winced at her rough treatment. "You're not safe until we do."

Our home ought to have been inviolate after the years of blood, sweat, and effort I had sank into the wards. But white witch work paled in comparison to the dark magical muscle the killer—or killers —was flexing.

"I don't want to be left behind again." She shrank to hair bow size. "No one will notice."

"I'll think about it." I squeezed past Clay and dropped her in the kitchen. "Eat your breakfast."

With a huff, she returned to normal size and set about making her usual meal. As slow as possible. There were snails in the flowerbeds moving faster than Colby as she eavesdropped on the adult conversations.

"Let me help you." I scooped up the bowl of pollen, made her fresh sugar water, then carried everything to her rig. She drifted behind me, barely flapping her wings, doing her best to drag her feet midair. "Stay put, and plug in. For real this time. There are some things you don't need to hear, okay? I don't want the images in your head."

"It's not like I haven't seen it before," she muttered softly. "I can handle it."

"You have, and you can." I swallowed to wet my throat. "That doesn't mean you should have to again."

Asa met me in the doorway with a grim expression that didn't bode well for our investigation.

"Nine agents have been present at all four crime scenes." He guided me into my chair then reclaimed his across from me. "Two of those, including Kidd, are junior agents. The rest are veterans." He checked the screen. "The Kellies are in the process of locating the seven we haven't spoken with yet."

"Okay." I rubbed my temples. "Why was Kidd recruited?"

"His mother was a lone wolf, and that's how she raised him." Clay knew the details without checking, so he must have already read this information. "She edged too close to the boundaries of her local pack's land when prey became scarce. Kidd trespassed during a hunt, the alpha heard about it, and he went to set Kidd straight. His mother recognized the alpha, panicked, and challenged him." Clay exhaled. "The alpha killed her quick. Kidd witnessed it. He flew into a rage, attacked and killed the alpha, then he ran."

A warg with alpha tendencies and the strength to overthrow a pack on a whim had to be kept in line.

Packs policed their own, but with Kidd a rogue, the pack must have called Black Hat to report him.

"That means he's strong, fast, and violent." A killer. Like the rest of us. "What else do we know?"

"He was a part-time film student at a local college and worked full-time for a techy big box store."

That fit with the artistic perspective Kidd brought to the crime scene videos and the possible camera hacking at the hotel.

"He has no magic." Asa worried one of his earrings. "If he's our copycat, then he's definitely one of a pair."

Wargs had only the magic they were born with. While it was transformation magic, it wasn't a gift they could share with others. They might eat hearts because they tasted good, but they wouldn't gain power from it. But souls? They had no means to call them or collect them, let alone consume them.

"The more we learn, the less we know." I stared at the ceiling. "I'm not a fan of playing defense."

Offense was more my style. Keep an opponent on their toes, and they had no time to plan their next steps.

The house phone rang, which was unusual, and I hopped up to answer. "Hello?"

"Are you back yet, dear?"

Miss Dotha's warm voice washed over me in a comforting wave. "I am."

She had called my house phone and not my cell phone, which meant I had to be home to answer, but I knew better than to sass her.

"Oh good." She drew in a deep breath. "I'm afraid I have bad news."

"Are you okay?" A ball of dread rolled in my gut. "Are the girls—?"

"It's nothing like that. We're all fine. It's your lovely store. It was broken into last night."

All at once, I could breathe again. "My store?"

"I called the police, and they've filed a report on the incident." She let me absorb that. "Are you there?"

"Yes." I hated my voice for cracking. "I'm here."

"Would you like to come down and see for yourself before I get my son to board up the front?"

"Yes." I sagged against the wall. "I'll be down there shortly. And thank you."

The call ended, but I stayed put, decisions churning through my head faster than I could make them.

"I need to handle this," I told the guys. "He might have left a nasty surprise for the cops to find."

The skull at the processor was a turning point in the killer's—or killers'—evolution.

From the mural on the cave wall, I had to assume this production was all for me. To get to Colby.

They wanted my attention, and now they had it.

"Serial killers don't change their spots." Clay exhaled. "Nothing about this case has made any sense since we brought you on board." He winced. "No offense." He stood. "We thought we had a copycat but..."

"The killer—" it was easier to think in the singular until we had hard evidence, "—did his homework. The Silver Stag was my last case, and he made a half-assed attempt at recreating it. He hit enough similarities to ensure the Bureau went searching for me. He let them do the legwork to find me then followed me to Colby."

Only an agent had the level of access required to learn the details of the Silver Stag case.

And only an agent had clearance for the systems storing the information on my whereabouts.

"How did he know about Colby?" Asa rose as well. "You were alone in the clearing."

"I don't know." I picked at my thumbnail. "I missed something or someone."

"Why would they wait ten years?" Clay shook his head. "It makes no sense."

"I don't know that either." I considered the timeline. "Ten isn't a powerful number. Seven or thirteen would have been better." I turned to Colby. "Ready to go, Hairbow?"

Without an ounce of shame, she shucked her headset, shrank, and landed on my head.

A smile twitched in Clay's cheek, but he wisely didn't bring up the total lack of discipline in my house.

The guys would have blended in better wearing casual clothes, but agents tended not to pack civvies.

Lucky for me, consultants got to wear what they wanted to work.

We piled into my sporty SUV, Clay swearing about tiny cars the whole way, and hit the road.

A rhythmic *boom, boom, boom* caused me to slow in front of Mrs. Gleason's house.

"Please don't be shotgun blasts," I murmured, hoping I wasn't about to become the party police.

The Yard Birds had flocked together, about a dozen of them, and you could never be too careful. Alcohol and firearms do *not* mix. Unless you're blending a murderita. But when I cracked my window, my fingers crossed, rap music pulsed in the air. I had been hearing the bass.

At least the massive hangover this promised Mrs. Gleason and her friends guaranteed that their eagle eyes would be too blurred to keep tabs on me.

For once, that would be a blessing.

Certain my neighbors were practicing safe keggering, I drove us into town and parked in the employee lot.

The three of us crossed to enter the store from the rear, and I paused with a hand on the knob.

Clay sidled up to me. "Want me to go first?"

I couldn't find my voice, so I shook my head and pushed inside before I lost my nerve.

A gasp escaped me at the total destruction of what had been a small dream come true.

Everything that could be broken had been, including the security cameras mounted in the corners.

Crunching over broken glass, I met a pair of officers at the front door who greeted me with curt nods.

We had a small police force, so their faces were familiar. Their name tags read Waters and Downy.

There was no sign of Miss Dotha or the girls. She must have driven them home after the police arrived.

"Ms. Hollis," Waters greeted me. "Do you have any enemies? Anyone who might want to hurt you?"

The abrupt questions shocked me into silence when I had been expecting the usual social niceties first.

"What he means is, this level of violence strikes us as personal." Downy cut his partner a sharp look then gentled his tone. "Do you have any idea who could have done this or why they targeted your store?"

The only choice I had was to stick to the lie I had been telling. "My ex-boyfriend."

"All right." Downy offered me a polite smile while he made notes. "What can you tell us about him?"

"Hold up, Downy." Waters cut into his partner's questioning to assess Asa and Clay. "Who are you two?"

"We're with Rue," Clay told him. "She let us in."

Asa did his best to appear as nonthreatening as possible, but Waters broke into a sweat looking at him.

"The man responsible for this mess is Neil Wells," I said loudly over Waters, then launched into my cover story for them both.

Neil Wells had existed, and he had been abusive to his girl-friends, but I had never been one of them. Black Hat put him down for blowing up a church to kill the vampires who slept in crypts beneath it. Why a selkie had it out for vampires, I had no idea, but Neil also managed to kill eight humans in the blast.

The director wasn't about to let that slip, since dead humans meant investigations that might expose the bones of creatures the Bureau didn't want to explain to mortal authorities. I figured Neil torched his reputation during his life, so I wasn't doing him harm by compounding his legacy after his death.

The police questioning dragged on for about thirty minutes, give or take, before Miss Dotha arrived on the scene.

"You boys have your answers." She shooed the officers out of the store. "Let the poor girl process."

The officers knew Miss Dotha at least as well as I did since neither of them opened their mouth to sass her.

And yes, Miss Dotha considered anything she didn't want to hear sass.

Gathering me into a fierce hug that smelled of lilacs, she patted my back, and the faint hum of distant magic in her blood soothed me. "There, there, dear."

Miss Dotha's affection was catlike, in that she gave it when she wanted, and she had claws.

Okay, so she had perfect oval-shaped acrylics, but they were digging into my skin, about to draw blood.

Something had rattled her. Not just the break-in. More personal than that. She was a tough woman, and she wouldn't be literally hanging on to me by her fingernails if there weren't more to the story than that.

When she didn't release me, I addressed the police over her shoulder. "We can take it from here."

"We'll be in touch," Downy assured me. "Call if you think of anything or if you see your ex in town."

"I'll do that," I told the polite lie. "Thank you for your service."

The officers left, and Miss Dotha's acrylic talons dug in deeper, but she didn't budge for a full minute.

"Miss Dotha." I couldn't extract myself without hurting her. "What's wrong?"

"He took them." Her arms began trembling around me. "He took the girls."

A lump formed in my throat. "Who?"

"Your ex." She pulled back but didn't let go. "He was here when I arrived at six. The weekly jar shipment came in last night, and I had inventory to do before we opened. The store was a mess, and when he saw me..." Tears filled her eyes. "He started ranting about a Colby Timms."

Tiny feet dug into my scalp while Colby panicked at the sound of her name on Miss Dotha's lips.

By this point, I was clutching her back. "What did he say about Colby?"

For him to bring Colby up to Miss Dotha, he must have sensed Miss Dotha's witch heritage and figured that was why I hired her. Smart as he was, he would have quickly realized he was mistaken to do so, that she was blissfully ignorant of my real identity. Frankly, I was amazed—and grateful—he let her live.

"He demanded to know where she was hiding or where she might go."

He must have thought she would run here after the house wards failed. "What did you tell him?"

"The truth." She stared up at me. "I've never heard of her." Her eyes were red-rimmed and puffy. "From what I know of your past, I assumed that was your birthname, that you changed it when you left him." A fresh wash of tears poured down her wrinkled cheeks. "He was about to leave when the girls arrived. He did something, I don't know what, but they collapsed in the doorway. Drugs, maybe? He had a stick with him. It was small, what my granny would call a switch. He couldn't have done all this damage with just it. He must have had help." She caught her breath. "He told me to call you and what to say."

And that, right there, was the reason she was still breathing. To play messenger.

"He took the girls with him?"

"Yes." She lowered her voice. "He picked them up, *both* of them, like they weighed nothing." Her bright eyes burned with fear. "As he walked out, the storefront began to crackle. I ran to the office to call you, just like he told me to do, and the glass exploded. He must have set up a bomb before I got here."

A bomb was as good of an excuse as any. "Did he tell you how to get in touch with him?"

"No." A sob broke free of her chest. "He said he would call with instructions."

Then he must be close. Watching. He would want to see I was following his rules.

"I need you to go home, pretend everything is normal, and help me keep the girls' parents in the dark." I regretted asking her to choose me over her own daughter, but Miss Dotha had overloaded her circuits. Bombs, superstrength, and possible drug use had tipped her over the edge. She was happy for simple directions. "I will call you the second I hear from the—" I bit down on the word *killer*, "—my ex."

Head down, Asa stepped up to Miss Dotha. "Can I drive you home, ma'am?"

Of the two agents, he fit behind the wheel easier, and without the risk of busting another seat.

"No thank you." Her hand rose to clutch her cross necklace. "The drive will give me time to calm down."

There was no correlation between Miss Dotha taking comfort in her religion and Asa's heritage, but he noticed the gesture and took a healthy step back. It made me wonder how often he garnered that reaction from those who were aware he was half daemon. With Clay as his partner, I doubt anyone mocked him twice.

As funny and sweet as Clay could be, he had a bad side no one in their right mind wanted to be on.

Clay took care of his people. It made me sound pathetic, but he had been my best friend. One of my only friends. I wasn't raised to search out others to form bonds. Aside from alliances. And those were iffy.

Clay had changed my life. Forever. He was the only person who had ever seen any good in me. He was as much to blame for the switch flipping in my head as Colby. Maybe he had been the true catalyst, his goodness priming me for the moment I said "Enough" as I sprouted a conscience of my own.

"Get our girls back." Miss Dotha cupped my cheek in her cold palm. "Kill the bastard who took them."

Humans spoke those words out of anger, not intent, but I wasn't human, and I meant to end this.

"Yes, ma'am," Clay answered for me. "We fully intend to do just that."

With that, Miss Dotha straightened her shoulders and crunched over glass until she hit the sidewalk.

Gesturing toward the office, I picked my way through the debris. "I'll check the phone."

"I'll call the Kellies," Clay said, "see if they can track Arden or Camber's cells."

The office was in ruins, the same as the store, but the portable phone worked when I lifted the handset.

"We're good to go." I scanned the mess. "This will be a nightmare to clean."

Lotions, bodywashes, tinctures, and more saturated the floor with a layer of slippery, smelly goop.

Whoever or whatever had been stealing my rosebuds, they were out of luck now.

And...yeah...that was the least important thing happening here, but the tiny details were easier to swallow than the big ones. Those, like filing insurance to repair my store, threatened to choke me.

Seeking out my furry hairbow, I stroked her back. "How are you holding up, Colby?"

"He took Camber and Arden..." her small voice trembled, "...because of me."

"No," Clay corrected her. "He took them because he's an asshole." He hesitated. "Butthole?"

The slip made her laugh, which I was sure had been the point, since he winked at me on the sly.

"None of this is your fault, smarty fuzz butt. From the start, you were an innocent in all this."

Nestling down in my hair, she hugged the top of my head and breathed, "Okay, Rue."

"Ms. Hollis?"

The voice drew me out to find the promised help in the form of Miss Dotha's son, Camber's uncle. "Hi, Clive."

"Mom told me you could use a hand." He whistled at the destruction. "I brought my boys and plywood."

"Thank you." I blamed the fresh tears on the overabundance of eucalyptus extract. "I'll pay for your time and your supplies." I met him at the door and shook his hand. "It's the least I can do."

"Mom would tan my hide if I let you do that." His smile was crooked. "I'm happy to help."

Two boys around fifteen or sixteen walked up with toolboxes in hand, and the three of them set to work boarding up the front of my shop, door and all, and sweeping the sidewalk clean to spare me the chore.

As much as I wanted to stalk the phone until it rang, I followed small town protocol and dialed the diner. I ordered my helpers, and the three of us, sandwiches and chips for an early lunch. It was the least I could do, even if the gesture felt empty. Miss Dotha had sent one of her sons to help, who had no clue his niece was missing. Her family was lending me a hand without any expectations *after* I had cost them so much.

No.

I couldn't think like that.

Camber and Arden would be okay.

They had to be.

About the time Clive and his boys finished up, I heard Ms. Hampshire call out a greeting.

I was still in the store, making a tiny dent in the mess, when she walked in with multiple bags hanging on her arms. They left bright white lines in her tan skin, and I rushed to take a few. Clay pitched in too, but I couldn't blame Asa for hanging back. He really did have a knack for spooking people. Especially humans.

"You didn't have to do this," I chided her. "I could have picked it up if you couldn't spare someone."

"Nonsense." She hugged me the second my hands were empty. "We all saw your poor shop."

"Yeah." I picked at a fingernail. "Miss Dotha sent her son and grandsons to help. Most of the food is for them."

"I figured." She glanced around the store. "Do you need help in here?"

"No." I gestured to my teammates. "The guys are helping me."

Asa had been sweeping and changing trash bags for me while Clay stood guard near the door.

The sight of Asa holding a broom and dustpan must have set Ms. Hampshire at ease.

In her world, the scary guys must not be domesticated.

"Oh good." She smiled at Clay and Asa. "Thank you both for helping our Rue."

"We're happy to, ma'am." Clay ducked his head. "Thank you for going out of your way for us."

"It's no problem." She waved him off. "Fresh air does a body good."

"How much do we owe you?" Clay pulled out his wallet. "Pass me that ticket, Rue."

"I won't take your money or hers." Ms. Hampshire lifted a hand. "Consider it a gift from me and Frank."

Outright refusal would hurt her feelings, and I had become a person who cared about others' feelings.

But that didn't mean I couldn't fuss. "You won't stay in business if you don't start charging people."

"Eh." She flipped that same hand. "I'm about to retire. Let the person who buys us out worry about it."

"Let me help you." Clay offered her his arm. "The floor is still slick in here."

"And they say chivalry is dead," she tittered. "Thank you, young man."

Clay was old as literal dirt, since he was made from the stuff, but he did look around forty.

Clive ducked his head into the store. "Are you ready for us to seal it up?"

"Yes." I passed him his bags of food. "Thank you all for your help today."

He grumbled to accept even that much payment, but the teens had their stomachs in their eyes.

Once Clay returned, Clive set the final sheet of plywood in place and began nailing it over the door.

"The Kellies replied." Clay shook his head. "The phones are both off. He can't track either of them."

The girls never turned their phones off, which meant the copycat had done it for them. "Last location?"

A slight hesitation told me how much he didn't want to say what came next. "Main Street."

The immediate powering down of the phones reaffirmed the killer was tech savvy, which truly sucked.

On the upside, the privacy allowed Colby to stretch her wings for the first time in hours, but she kept her perch on my head. Pretty sure she had been asleep and had gone right back to napping to pass the time.

The wood blocked us from view off Main Street, and I deflated a bit, as if this version of me, this Rue, had been punctured with a sharp needle. Past and present, the two halves of my life had collided right out of the gate. I had been a fool to think I could keep this part untainted by the darkness of the other.

Black Hat was a cancer in its agents, and I was proof there was no cure.

15

The phone rang.

Ten hours and change after we arrived at the store.

I had been staring at it, willing its display to light. For a panicked heartbeat, I couldn't decide if it was real or wishful thinking. The handset slipped across my damp palm when I grabbed it and answered.

"Hollis Apothecary, Rue Hollis speaking."

Asa ducked into the office, mop in hand. Clay was right behind him. Both were listening in.

So was Colby, who was cuddled into a jacket Arden had left in the office, her dark eyes wide with worry.

"You have something I want," a quiet, male voice informed me. "And I have two somethings you want."

"You'll have to be more specific."

"I want the loinnir." He paused. "Give it to me, and I will return the girls I took from your store."

The long wait had cured me of any urge to play games. "I want proof of life."

Twin screams pierced the air behind the caller, and he sucked in a breath, as if savoring their pain.

In a blink, Colby shot off the desk, shrank, and nested down until my hair hurt from her yanking on it.

"There is your proof of life." His voice grew huskier. "Meet me at Tadpole Swim."

The lack of qualifiers stumped me. "When?"

A soft laugh flavored his tone. "Now."

The call ended before I could ask more questions. No doubt that was the point.

"He didn't tell me to come alone." I flung the phone at its base. "That's not a good sign."

Villains loved their catchphrases, and that had to be number one.

Maybe number two, right behind *don't call the cops.*

Which, now that I thought about it, he hadn't used that line on Miss Dotha either.

"He knows you won't come alone." Clay didn't sound worried one bit. "Why bother lying about it?"

Apparently, he appreciated a criminal willing to cut through the BS to the meat of the problem.

"He wanted off the phone as fast as possible," Asa murmured. "Check the caller ID."

"Maybe he worried we used our spare time to tap the line." Clay shrugged. "Paranoia does that."

Magic created too many loopholes for old school tech to be anywhere near reliable in these situations.

"He used Arden's cellphone. It's on. It's turned on." A drum beat in my chest. "Call the Kellies."

There was every reason to believe the copycat had used a spell to conceal his location, but hope was like a weed. Hard to kill.

"We need to move." I pushed from the desk and stood. "They'll have to track on the way."

Clay left the call to Asa. "How far is this Tadpole thing?"

"About twenty minutes outside town. It's a popular swimming hole for teens."

The girls met their boyfriends up there in summer, sneaking around like they invented skinny-dipping.

We burst out the back of the store, and I didn't bother locking up behind us. We climbed in my SUV, and I drove the exact posted speed limit to give the Kellies more time to hit us with some good news.

"What will we do when we get there?" Colby's quiet voice rang clear in the silence.

"Not hand you over, if that's what you're thinking."

A shiver rippled through her I pretended not to feel. "You love Camber and Arden too, so..."

"I do, but me and you?" I reached up to scratch her head. "We're in this together."

"Okay." She nestled back down. "I believe you."

"You better." I glared at her in the rearview mirror. "Or I'll have to spank your fuzzy butt."

A teeny-tiny laugh escaped her, and it was good enough for me. The kid didn't deserve this. She survived the Silver Stag, but she lost everything. Her life, her family, herself. She got stuck as a moth. For eternity. Now her very existence was a temptation to those who practiced dark arts.

It wasn't fair to force her down memory lane, but life wasn't fair. Never had been, never would be.

About ten minutes out, Asa's phone rang, and we all held our collective breath.

"They have a general area," he reported, then waited on the line. "They have a location, one mile east."

"No wonder he didn't bother concealing himself," I muttered. "He was calling on his way to Tadpole."

"Probably," Clay agreed. "What's our plan?"

"There's no time for a plan." Asa stared out his window. "We don't even know who or what to expect."

Hard to plan a strategy with so many unknowns up in the air. "We'll wing it."

Colby stomped several of her tiny feet on my head. "I hope that wasn't a moth joke."

As much as I wanted to smile at her attitude coming back to her, I couldn't get my mouth to cooperate.

"The black witch will be there," I said instead. "As to the who, I guess we're about to find out."

Might be Kidd, might be something that looked like Kidd. Might be whoever cut off Olsen's face.

Variables were endless, but our time had run out. The killer had his goal in sight and wanted to score.

I parked where the pavement ended, and we sat there while I lined up my thoughts.

"Clay." I held my hand out to Colby, she climbed on, and I passed her to him. "Protect her at all costs."

Burnt-crimson eyes bored into me. "Who's going to protect you?"

"I can take care of myself." I twitched my lips in a smile Asa didn't appreciate. "But I wouldn't mind if you followed me in, say, five minutes. That's how long it will take me to get to the pond."

His lips parted, but whatever he planned to say died on a soft exhale of breath.

"Colby, listen to Clay." I twisted to face her. "Do whatever he tells you, okay?"

"Be careful, Rue." She climbed up his arm to sit on his shoulder. "Promise."

"Cross my heart." I made the motion. "And cross your fingers."

I slid out before I lost my nerve, shut my door like it would protect them, then set off down the path.

The pond was how I remembered it the one time Miss Dotha sent me to fetch Camber after a missed curfew. It wasn't wide, but it was deep. It saw too much action for scum to thrive on the surface, but a green tint colored the water when sunlight hit it just right. Tonight, with the new moon, the water loomed as black as pitch.

"You did an admirable job of hiding." The same quiet voice from the phone rode on a warm breeze. "I'm embarrassed how long it took me to find you."

As far as I could tell, I was alone, but I heard him clear as a bell. "You didn't find me, though."

"True." Distaste twisted the word. "I was forced to get creative."

"Creative?" I aimed straight for his artist's ego. "You think killing all those girls makes you *creative?*"

"The Silver Stag went down in history as one of the most notorious serial killers of our time, but that title was earned on sheer numbers alone. There was no art in what he did. There was only hunger for power. But he lacked the stomach for the job. He transformed his prey into animals to strip them of humanity."

"Nice theory." I tried homing in on his voice. "I read his profile too."

A crow's loud cawing rent the night and blasted shivers down my spine.

"I elevated his primitive methodology but was forced to retain certain key aspects to guarantee that the director would reach out to you. See, I had a theory. I believed the director knew exactly where you disappeared to all those years ago. But he proved resistant to involving you. I had to resurrect the killer all fae parents had come to fear in order to force his hand, and here you are."

"You got me." I spread my hands. "Now what do you want?"

"Colby Timms."

From high above me, mocking laughter rained down from the crow.

Normal crows didn't laugh in perfect sync with villain monologues. "Nice familiar you've got there."

The killer wasn't in the mood to be distracted, but all I had to do was find the right topic. Talking kept him from wrapping this up, and that was the best I could do until Asa got in place. Backup wouldn't cure all my woes, but it would give me a morale boost to know I wasn't alone.

"Why the processor?"

"Hearts aren't the only parts of the body rich in nutrients and power. Thaddeus has a taste for livers."

The crow squawked in eager agreement, or at the sound of his name. Either way, it was creepy as heck.

Wrong topic.

This one made my stomach turn when I needed to be ice cold, not fever hot with rage for his victims.

"Why wait ten years to get *creative* with finding me?"

"I invested several years in staging my death. The director is a cautious man, and he held my true name. I had to be careful when I orchestrated a fitting end in the line of duty so that I would be clear for recruitment under a new face. I would have preferred thirteen years, as I'm sure you would have guessed, but I grew impatient."

"You made mistakes."

"Agent Kidd noticed Thaddeus was present in all his *films*. I got close to Kidd, to determine what he knew, but I overplayed my hand. He began to suspect me. I had no way of knowing if he shared his suspicions with anyone else, and I couldn't risk it. He hadn't been in the system long. He was eager to please. Eager to belong. He thought the Bureau would provide him with a surrogate pack."

A twist in my chest allowed the floodgates of guilt to swing wide open.

His use of the past tense told me all I needed to know about Kidd.

He was dead.

The copycat had killed him.

And we hadn't even tried to save him.

I wrote Kidd off as a bad apple at the first opportunity then left him to rot in the barrel.

One more sin added to my black soul that I would never wash clean.

"That bird..." Pieces of the puzzle snicked together in my head. "You sent it to harass Colby."

"My familiar," he corrected me. "With you away, there was no harm in him testing your defenses."

"With the added benefit of scaring the bejesus out of Colby," I snarled, too late to quiet my rage.

With that outburst, I told him all he needed to know about our relationship. She wasn't only a familiar. It wasn't just her magic that made her special to me. He knew now I cared about her. I *loved* her. And that made me more vulnerable than I was already. Gone was any hope of convincing him she was a means to an end. I might have sold him on me using her as a power source otherwise, but my heart spoke loudest.

Life had been so much easier when I lived like I didn't have one, didn't need one, didn't want one.

"Colby Timms," he repeated. "You brought her with you. I can sense her. Where is she?"

Wings fluttering over my head made me twitchy, but I held my ground. "How did you know about her?"

"Thaddeus told me."

The big-mouth bird squawked at the compliment, and I understood my mistake. "You were there."

"I was a senior agent, but I wore my true face then. I got called in as backup along with my partner." A scratching noise warned me the crow was still above me. "I sent my familiar ahead to scout the location. I can see through his eyes when I choose, and what I witnessed that night changed everything."

Everything had changed. He was right about that. But it changed for all of us, changed *us*, not just him.

"I thought you would consume the loinnir, I expected no less from a Báthory, but you didn't. You tucked that little moth girl in your pocket and vanished without a trace. I thought at first you meant to feast on her in private, but I scented your magic at the scene. You bonded her to you. Saved her. She's your familiar."

Limbs shook overhead as the blasted crow took flight, and it leaving was somehow worse than it staying.

The scabs over my heart bled to recall that night. "Where are Arden and Camber?"

"The humans?" He hesitated. "I did promise to return those to you, didn't I?"

"You did."

"You know what I want in exchange."

"Show yourself," I ordered instead. "I'm tired of talking to shadows."

An unassuming young man stepped from behind a tree too thin to shield him without magical help. I had only seen him once, for a few minutes at the third crime scene as I unraveled the spell, but I recognized him.

David Taylor.

The junior agent Kidd introduced to me as Taylor wasn't a warg after all, but I bet the real one had been.

The masque Taylor wore emitted the same paranormal frequency as its original owner. It was enough to fool most people. Me included. If you didn't know to look.

"There were two possibilities for how this would end," Taylor said with an air of resignation. "You were this great and terrible creature once. Men trembled before you. You were a feral and depraved beast contained in the skin of a woman." He wet his lips. "I idolized you. When Black Hats came for me, I let them take me. I wanted to join the Bureau, to be your right hand, but you broke before I got the chance."

"Who were you?" I squinted at him, knowing it would tell me nothing. "I don't remember you."

"Everyone was beneath your notice then." He smiled in remembrance. "Gods, you were a sight."

A hollow sensation carved out my stomach as another thought occurred to me, worse than the others.

"You targeted Colby to punish me," I realized. "Did my defection wipe the stars from your eyes?"

"Yes," he growled, stepping closer to the water. "As a matter of fact, it did."

Sparks ignited in his palms, dark purple and midnight blue, and he raised his arms out to his sides.

"You taught me a valuable lesson." He shot a bolt of magic at my feet, and I leapt back with my boot tips singed. "No matter how humble or highborn our origins, we can rise above them...or sink below them."

The magic he was tossing around far outclassed what I had on tap, but I palmed my wand all the same.

"Ah." I kept on my toes as his strikes landed closer and closer. "Tender about our humble origins, are we?"

He was wearing me down. I knew that. He would keep me dancing until he decided to cut my strings.

Colby would be free of her familiar bond then, and her soul would leave her body.

There was no doubt in my mind he planned to consume it, consume *her*, as I died bearing witness.

The pointed caw of a crow drew his attention skyward, and he held out his hand.

A hank of long, black hair slid through his fingers. In the dark, it dripped black and slick like blood.

The bottom fell out of my stomach at the sight of Asa's beautiful hair.

"Your daemon won't interrupt us." He let the wind take the strands. "The golem, however, is nine feet behind you to your left. Thaddeus tells me he has the loinnir with him. Kind of him, to bring her to me."

I whirled around to find nothing but forest behind me, and I had only seconds to grasp my mistake.

A bolt of magic struck the top of my head like lightning and zinged through my body into the ground.

Coughing up smoke and blood, I hit my knees, and Taylor was on me in a heartbeat.

"Think of it like this..." he fisted my hair and cranked my head back until our eyes met, "...your death will seal your reputation. Your legacy will survive untarnished by this pathetic attempt at redemption."

From the moment Miss Dotha whispered in my ear, I had known my troubles would be over tonight.

A white witch couldn't beat him. *I* couldn't beat him. Unless I was willing to die for it.

And take Colby with me.

Had she been here to ask, I knew the path my brave girl would have chosen.

Fingers tightening on my wand, I began a low chant that swelled in volume until the warmth of my power filled me to over-flowing. Light blossomed under my skin, the glow a beautiful white that swelled until it spilled from my pores in a pulse that blinded me.

"Stop." He cupped my jaw, seconds from snapping my neck. "You can't defeat me."

He was wrong, and I was about to prove it to him with deadly consequences for us both.

"Rue might not be able to defeat you," Clay rumbled at Taylor, "but she can."

She? *She?* The only *she* in his care had no business charging to my rescue.

I would strangle Clay for this. I would have to survive it first, yeah, but then it was on.

Why on Earth would he bring Colby straight to the man whose obsession had cost so many lives?

A featherlight touch anointed my forehead, and more of that sweet, bright power flooded me.

The brightness in me hadn't been my burgeoning death curse burning up my throat. It was all her.

Of all the hearts I had eaten, none had given me this potent rush. It left me...cleansed...somehow.

And terrified to my core what I might be willing to do to feel this way again.

"Me and you." Colby's soft feet brushed tears from my cheeks. "We're in this together."

"You..." I breathed as my vision cleared. "Your power is doing this."

Colby shone, radiant and powerful, a star fallen to earth.

"It's us." She fed more of her strength into me. "*We* can do this."

"Gods," Taylor marveled. "I knew she would be magnificent."

Releasing my hair, he swooped his hands in to cup Colby and scoop her off my face.

The tips of his fingers burned when he touched her wings, and he howled with rage.

Freed of his clutches, I braced Colby with a hand then rolled aside to put distance between us and Taylor.

"Where are the girls?" The wand singed my palm. "What have you done with them?"

"Give me the loinnir," he snarled, fingers curling into his palms. "She was never meant to be yours."

"Colby belongs to herself," I informed him. "She just lets me hang with her."

Incredulity darkened his eyes, and he flung out his ruined hands to summon more electric magic.

Heat engulfed every inch of my skin, tightening it until I felt ready to burst, and then I shattered.

A wave of power blasted out of me, washing through the clearing and immolating Taylor.

The world turned white and too bright for my eyes, but I willed my vision to return, panic coasting down my spine. I wanted to see Taylor's ashes. I wanted to kick them. But mostly I wanted to know beyond the shadow of a doubt that he was dead, and Colby was safe from him.

Sweaty and shaky, I sank to my knees to keep from tipping over onto my face.

As shape and color returned, I located the pile of gray dust and breathed a sigh of relief.

Colby, still in beacon mode, shone from the tree limb over my head while she kept watch over me.

"Okay, glowworm." I threw up a hand to shield my eyes. "Dial it down a few notches."

"How cool is this?" She twirled in the air. "I'm totally a light mage."

"Very cool." Clay stepped up beside me. "You're absolutely a light mage."

Too bad her MMRPG friends could never know what a true badass they played alongside.

"Yes, well, use your newfound powers for good." I squinted less as she dimmed. "Do you hear...?"

An earsplitting caw lodged my heart in my throat. *Thaddeus.* I had forgotten about him.

"Come here." I held my hand out over my head. *"Now."*

Too late.

I was too late.

Fast as a bullet, Thaddeus swooped toward Colby, his aim perfect.

"Colby."

Flaring his wings at the last minute, Thaddeus slowed his descent and extended his taloned feet.

A thickly muscled arm shot up as the crow closed in and yanked it out of the air in a tight fist.

With a bestial roar in its face, the daemon that was Asa bit off its head with a crunch.

Colby, distracted by the daemon, smacked into the side of my face then slid down onto my shoulder, where it was safe.

Relief that had nothing to do with having Colby warm and safe in my arms shuddered through me.

Asa was okay. Better than okay, he was *alive*. He was...really going to town on that crow.

"You're scaring the kid," Clay warned him. "Spit that out and throw the rest away."

The daemon growled low in its throat, chewed a few more times, then sighed and did as he was told.

Adrenaline could only keep you going for so long. As it flushed out my system, I was forced to accept the truth that my actions carried terrible consequences. Taylor was dead, as in pile-of-ash dead, and we had no idea where he'd stashed Arden and Camber. He had held them captive for ten-plus hours. It was far too easy for me to imagine what he might have done to the girls during that time, what he left for us to find.

"Where do we start?" I spun toward Clay. "What did the Kellies say?"

They hadn't gotten back with us before I went to meet Taylor, but any location information they gave us was more critical now than ever.

The girls were on all sorts of social apps that fed their location information to their friends and followers. For once, I was grateful they had ignored Miss Dotha's—and my—warnings about making them so easy to find. Surely Taylor wouldn't have bothered disabling them when he called me right to him.

"Fan out." I made a circular motion with my finger. "Let's search the perimeter for any surprises."

We broke apart and combed the area. Aside from a rusted chain strung from a limb that hung into the water, we found nothing in the immediate area. The chain was peppered with rotting wooden dowels. Teens swung from it over the water then let go with a splash. It had been here last time, and I saw firsthand how it was used then.

After we regrouped, I told them, "We need to search the spot where Taylor called me from."

I didn't have to remind them of the screams he offered as proof of life. They would have heard them.

"Agreed." Clay began walking, phone in hand. "It will give the Kellies time to work."

Asa elected to remain in his daemon form. How he kept his thick horns and hair, which was too thick to tell me if he had a bald spot, from snagging on low-lying limbs mystified me. He moved with an easy grace through the trees that could only stem from his fae heritage.

"Here." He thrust a hank of his long hair at me. "Pet."

"I have other things on my mind right now." I swatted his hand. "No thanks."

"Pet," he growled at me. "Now."

On my shoulder, Colby snickered and snorted with no attempt to hide her laughter.

"Fine." I held the lock of hair like a leash and kept searching. "Happy?"

The daemon rumbled and puffed out his chest as if me leading him around was the best thing ever.

The hike took no time, but the coordinates gave nothing away. Nothing but trees, trees, and more trees.

"Everyone, stand clear." I used the excuse to return the daemon's hair to him. "I'm going to—"

"*We.*" An insistent foot tapped on top of my head. "We are going to...whatever you were about to say."

"Colby..."

"Don't *Colby* me." She stomped again. "I'm your familiar." Her voice softened. "Let me help you. Please, Rue."

After everything she had been through, I should have known how much it mattered to her that she help break the cycle. She didn't want any other girls to end up like her or worse. And I...I had to respect that.

"Okay." I took out my wand. "We're going to douse the area for residual magic."

"Ready." Her wings fluttered overhead. "Let's do this." She sank to my eye level. "How do we do this?"

"I'll use a spell." I exhaled my frustration. "You can feed me a *tiny* bit of power to extend my range."

"I can do that." She blinked a few times. "I think."

At the pond, she had acted on instinct. Fear for me had guided her. This was different. It required intent.

"Don't sweat it." I smiled at her. "You've already saved the day. I don't mind pulling my own weight."

The praise lit her up from the inside. Not literally this time. Thankfully. I needed to see what I was doing.

Eyes shut tight, I held my wand in a loose grip and chanted under my breath while turning a slow circle. I made one full rotation before nodding to Colby, who zipped over to land on top of my head. She gripped my hair with her hands and began to hum a little ditty.

No.

She wasn't humming.

Her power was buzzing along her body and vibrating through mine in an audible harmonization.

Shutting my eyes again, I dowsed for signs of magic. A quiver shot down my arm, alerting me to residual energies. Taylor had concealed whatever spell he cast, but Colby's light magnified its stain on the earth. I focused on Camber and Arden, their faces, their voices, their laughter, and swept my arm in a wider arc.

A pulse shot up my arm, straight to my heart, and I gasped as my eyes opened on a new direction.

"We just came from there." Clay rubbed his nape. "Are you sure you're not picking up on the fight?"

A lot of magic had been thrown around near the pond. It was a miasma of dark and light energies.

"Probably." I rubbed my face with my hands. "Any word from the Kellies?"

"I'm sorry." Colby snuggled against my scalp. "I thought I could help."

"You did help." I patted her. "Your magic is unlike anything I've ever felt. I must be channeling it wrong."

"We'll figure it out." She crept forward then leaned over my forehead. "We're a team now, right?"

"Taylor held the girls captive for hours before he called," Clay cut in, sparing me from explaining to Colby how tonight made it that much more dangerous for people to discover her existence. "What was he doing?"

"The magic here is faint." I thought about how it felt. "He might have been meditating."

Black witches tended to require time to come back to themselves after large expenditures of power.

That, or the darkness they unleashed within themselves turned them stark raving mad.

"What was he doing at the pond?" Clay glanced back the way we had come. "For eight hours?"

The better question was what had he done there to expend so much power he had to recenter himself.

"Nothing good," the daemon rumbled. "Go back?"

"I'm going to dowse and walk." I pointed to each of them. "Don't let me smack into a tree."

"Where's the trust?" Clay laughed. "You know I won't let you kiss bark."

Allowing my eyes to close, I extended my arms and addressed Colby. "Ready?"

Wings aflutter, she yelled, "Ready."

Careful not to burn her out, I modulated the flow of power from Colby into me, and we got to work.

Deep within my casting, I was aware of the occasional nudge or bump to prevent me from crashing, but I ignored the physical contact to focus on the destination. Until a wide palm wrapped around my arm and stopped my forward motion with gentle insistence that caused me to open my eyes.

We had arrived.

And by *arrived*, I meant we had walked a perfect circle right back to where we started at the pond.

The daemon holding on to me studied the area but shrugged when he discovered nothing new.

"Don't let me tip into the water," I told him, then nudged Colby. "Let's dial up the juice."

"Okay." She jittered with excitement. "I'm ready."

Before I got my arm lifted, she channeled a flood of white light through me that spat out my wand to fizz and pop on the surface of the pond. I honed my focus, but her power was insistent. We had found them.

Calling upon my will, I broke the connection between Colby and me then staggered back.

"They're in the pond." I wiped my sweaty palms on my pants. "There was too much residual energy after the battle for me to sense them, but this is it. The girls are here. They have to be." I hit my knees in the mud. "I can't believe…"

A firm hand landed on each of my shoulders as Clay and the daemon comforted me.

Grief roiling through me, I tipped back my head to stare at the night sky and spotted the rusty chain.

"You don't think…?" I lurched back to my feet and fisted its taut length. "We have to check."

Until we exhausted all leads, we weren't going anywhere. I couldn't face Miss Dotha or the girls' parents otherwise. The girls couldn't have survived this long underwater without help, but Taylor was a skilled witch. There were several ways he could have submerged them long term while keeping them alive to use as bargaining chips, and that would explain where he spent his magic.

"There's tension on it." Clay sounded surprised. "The way it hangs into the water makes it hard to tell."

The thick links made for a sturdy but heavy chain one of the teens must have pilfered from a parent.

"Pull," the daemon told him, gripping the chain. "For Rue."

The guys put their backs into hauling the chain out of the murky pond, link by slimy link, while I kept a wary eye on the water for any traps Taylor might have set. Colby peered over my head, helping, though I wanted nothing more than to send her up to a high limb to watch from there or even back to my SUV.

But the familiar was out of the bag now. Good luck stuffing her back in it. I would have to allow Colby to make her own decisions about how—and *if*—she used her powers. To rob her of choice would make me as bad or worse than the Stag or Taylor.

"It's stuck." Clay braced his legs. "There's definitely something down there bumping the sides."

"Then I'm going in." I lifted Colby in the air. "I hope there aren't leeches." I shuddered. "Colby, you're my lookout." I stripped down to my bra and panties, grateful the daemon saw the floorshow instead of Asa. "Guys, I'm going to lower myself using the chain. Don't panic if you feel it jerking." I hesitated. "Actually, do panic if you feel it jerking, but light wiggling is fine."

"Bad idea," the daemon grumbled. "New plan."

"We don't know what shape the girls are in." I refused to voice my darkest worries. "I have to do this."

"She's right." Clay looped extra chain around his fist for a better grip. "The time to act is now."

Taking his advice to heart, I followed the chain into the water, my hand sliding over the slick links. Fear I might drop my wand into the abyss forced me to leave it behind, but I wasn't happy about it. After murmuring a spell for illumination in the hopes the burning globe would light my way, I filled my lungs with air and let myself sink.

Hand over hand, I hauled myself into the darkness with my eyes slitted against the filth of the water.

The ball of light drifted slowly ahead of me, but visibility was low. I didn't see the cage until my guide dipped between its wooden bars and bounced off a pale shoulder.

Scooping the light into my palm, I shone it side to side until I located a thick root piercing the enclosure. I braced a hip on the wall, dug my toes into the muck to brace myself, then jiggled until the cage jerked free.

Once I verified it was clear of entanglements, I gave two hard pulls to signal to the guys I was done.

A hard yank knocked me into the opposite wall as the cage shot past me. Shoving off the packed mud, I hooked my fingers into the bottom of the cage and rode it all the way to the surface.

The second air hit my face, the daemon was there, his arm an iron band around my waist as he dragged me to shore.

Coughing and spluttering, I watched Clay secure the chain to hold the cage above the water.

Now that I could see the whole picture, I wish I hadn't opened my eyes.

Camber and Arden huddled together, their fingers laced, and their heads bowed until their hair tangled.

"Are they...?" Clay stepped into the water. "Did you check for a pulse?"

"No," I rasped, my throat sore like I had been screaming. Maybe I had been.

Slow to leave my side, the daemon joined Clay in pulling the cage onto shore and unhooking it.

"There's no door." Clay scratched his head. "The bottom must be hinged."

On trembling legs, I stood and joined them. Upon closer exami-nation of the cage, I wanted to kill Taylor all over again. "He grew it around them."

There were no hinges, no seams, no doors. No escape. The entire piece had been twisted from roots and vines that had slithered under and around the girls until it finished weaving the spoked dome over them.

No wonder they had been screaming. They were terrified. He had sealed them in and made me listen.

The spell he used on the fae girls he preyed on wouldn't work on humans. Their souls were too faint, too ephemeral, to make consuming them worthwhile unless there was no other food source available.

But there were petrification spells, freeze spells, sleep spells, any number of vicious options that killed their target, if they remained in stasis for too long. Hard to believe, but those were the best-case scenarios.

Before I understood her intent, Colby flew between the bars to land on Camber's shoulder.

Eyes shut, wings flexing, Colby's power lit her tiny body.

"They're alive." She shot up over to me. "I don't know what's wrong, though."

Sweet relief crashed through me. "We can work with that."

"Want me to crack it open?" Clay tested the bars. "They seem flexible enough."

"Yes." I didn't waste more time dressing, just retrieved my wand. "We need it off them."

The daemon gripped two thick vines and strained with all his might. They bent, but they didn't break.

Clay tried his luck, but he might as well have been wrestling with a ball of rubber bands.

"It must be part of the spell." I touched my wand to a vine for a reading. "It's *definitely* part of the spell."

"Rue." Clay rushed to my side. "Don't move."

Heart kicking up, I froze in place as he cupped my shoulder. Jerking my head toward his hand, I watched as Colby's legs buckled. The stubborn girl hadn't warned me she was fading, but Clay had been keeping an eye on her. She slid off me into his waiting palm with a sigh and didn't so much as twitch afterward.

"Colby." I grasped his hand, yanking it to me, certain my worst fears had come true. "Are you...?"

I knew I shouldn't let her help. I *knew* it. But I did it anyway. I even *liked* it.

No, no, no.

"She's asleep." He smiled softly down at her. "Her battery is empty."

For several long seconds, I watched to be sure she was breathing easy. "I think you're right."

"Of course I'm right." He cradled her gently. "Look, I've known a lot of familiars in my time. A hundred or more. I've seen burnout before. Many times. This might be my first loinnir, but I'm telling you that's what this is." He scanned the pond. "She threw around a lot of magic. Probably discharged an accumulation since she's never functioned in her familiar capacity."

The cage waited beyond, but this was Colby. "You're sure...?"

"I'm sure." He held her close in a gesture of protection. "I've got her. You work on the girls."

"Let me grab my kit." I needed all the help I could get without Colby. "I should be able to do this solo."

The idea of leaving the girls stuck as they were until Colby recovered was out of the question.

I started by pouring a salt circle around them and sealing it with three drops of my blood. From there, I burnt herbal offerings in a cauldron the size of my palm. I lit a bundle of dragon's blood sage for potency and protection and walked a slow circuit around the cage, filling the air with its heady smoke and earthy fragrance. A few blood crystals placed and blessed at the four corners gave me another boost.

I just hoped it was enough.

With enough preparation time, I could work minor miracles even on my new diet. I prayed to any and all gods and goddesses who listened that this unraveling revived the girls, but they rarely favored me. I made my own luck.

Pressure built behind my breastbone in stark contrast to the easy flow I channeled earlier, but this magic came from me. It was all mine. What remained of it. I could do this, but it would cost me. Lucky for me, I had Clay here to catch me if I fell. And, though ours was a new and tenuous trust, Asa too.

And his daemon.

He would probably save me for the sake of having someone to pet him.

As my chant built to a crescendo, I aimed my wand and unleashed my counterspell on the circle with a tap.

A beat before my eyes rolled back in my head, I swore I heard twin inhales that exhaled on screams.

16

A familiar scent roused me from sleep. Tobacco. And...green apples?

From deeper in the house, Colby barked orders while she battled orcs with her friends. But a rhythmic *click, click, click* kept steady time at my elbow. That was not part of the game, and they only ever played one.

Cracking my eyes open, I discovered Asa sitting in a chair stolen from the kitchen beside my bed. Rimless glasses perched on his nose, and the beginnings of a scarf poised on a pair of wooden knitting needles.

A tiny part of me wondered if that was what he had been whittling in my yard that day, but I didn't ask.

"Am I dreaming?" I angled my head to see him better. "You wear glasses? And knit?"

"We all need our hobbies." He set aside his project. "Stakeouts are boring." He removed his glasses. "It's not that I need these to see. I need them to see *beyond*." He leaned forward. "Tinkkit is an ancient fae craft my mother taught me. I knit intent into my work, and my daemon half has trouble perceiving the strands of the natural positive energy I channel. The spelled glass helps me block out my daemon sight."

"You're a fascinating dae, Asa." I wiped the crust from my eyes. "Maybe one day you could..."

A gasp caught in my chest as it all rushed back to me, and I bolted upright, my heart racing a mile a minute.

"Shh." He gripped my upper arms to hold me still. "The girls are alive and well and in the hospital."

A twist in my middle left me tasting bile. "The hospital?"

"They're being treated for exposure and shock." He stroked his thumbs over my arms. "The spell hit the girls hard, and they hadn't shaken it off when the paramedics arrived. That type of magic isn't meant for use on humans, so it was in their best interest to be examined by human health professionals."

Wetting my lips, I screwed up my courage. "What do they remember...?"

"Not much." He gave me a reassuring squeeze. "They were unconscious for most of it."

"You interviewed them."

As much as I wished he hadn't asked them to relieve their trauma, he had no choice. I had explained him away as a cop, so the girls would have trusted him. They would have answered his questions without the trepidation that came from a formal interrogation. That much, I had done right. I still didn't like it.

"I had to know what precautions to take." He flexed his jaw, as if he regretted the necessity. "I gave both of the girls a dose of a mild potion to blur the edges of their memories. That ought to protect them."

From Black Hat. From the director. From a truth that would wreck and ruin them.

"Thank you," I rasped, grateful beyond measure for his quick thinking.

Agents kept an emergency tin of potions in their cars, a magical first aid kit, but the pre-mixed spells had a shelf life and required immediate application to be effective. That wasn't always possible, and humans died because what they had seen or heard couldn't be blurred, smudged, or faded in time to save them.

"Colby?" Her steady voice assured me she was all right, but I had to know if she was okay. "How is she?"

"Clay was right." Asa slid his hands down to my elbows. "She was exhausted, but she's fine."

His assurance shoved a weight off my shoulders, and I shut my eyes to soak in the fact I hadn't hurt her.

This time. Next time? I didn't want to think about it. But I knew Colby was sizing us for matching superhero costumes in her mind.

"We found Taylor's car." Asa let me go, and I missed his steadying grip. "This was inside."

A heavy weight landed on my lap, and I popped my eyes open to find a pale leather grimoire.

"There's a part, near the back, that might help you put everything into perspective."

"You read it?" I felt dirty just holding it. "You didn't read it aloud, right?"

"Black arts don't bother me much. Daemon, remember?" His smile was tolerant. "And I'm no fool."

"Sorry." I touched his shoulder. "I didn't mean to imply..."

"I understand your caution." He tilted his head, listening. "I'm going to tell the others you're awake."

"Thank you." I caught his hand as he stood. "I mean it."

Without another word, he bent and brushed his warm lips across my suddenly hot and tingly cheek.

Shoving handsome agents who knitted out of my mind, I cracked open the grimoire to a marked page.

I read the passage, reread the passage, then well and truly felt like a fool of the highest order.

What I did to Colby wasn't an accident. It was a conscious decision. For us both. But I never intended her to fulfil her role as my familiar. Therefore, I didn't study her rare condition, our unique bond, or anything else to do with what happened that night. We both chose to pretend this was how we had always been.

Last night—I assumed it was last night?—proved that ignorance was not bliss.

According to the grimoire, Taylor hypothesized that since I bound Colby to me at the height of my power that she would have a greater capacity for storing and channeling magic. But she was a soul given form. An *innocent* soul. The rarest and most powerful kind. Children of a certain age were often targeted by supernatural predators for that exact reason. In binding Colby, I had caught pure lightning in a bottle.

And, according to the numerous spells outlined in the grimoire, anyone could pop her cap and drink.

All they had to do was kill me first so that our bond would release Colby's soul.

As I flipped deeper into the book, I discovered the complex spell Taylor used for creating his masque and worse. Far worse. Curses. Enchantments. Soul magic.

The door burst open on cat-size Colby and Clay, and I shoved the grimoire under my pillow.

I took a moth right between the eyes as she smacked into my face and clung tight to my hair.

"You're awake." Her furry body jittered as she slid down to stare at me. "You slept a *lot* longer than me."

"Go ahead." I peeled her off and plonked her on my lap. "Mock me with your supreme powers."

For a moth, she did smug well. "I thought I just did."

"Are you sure you're okay?" I examined her. "You're not hurt or feeling puny or anything?"

"I feel like I drank the whole tub of sugar water in one gulp."

"Um..." I glanced at Clay, our resident familiar expert. "Is that normal?"

"The more power a familiar channels, the more power they're able to channel." He shrugged. "Colby is already a powerhouse. She's only going to grow stronger the more you work with her." He hesitated. "The cork is out of the bottle, so to speak. Now that Colby has used her powers in conjunction with yours, she has to keep expending the energy her body will naturally begin to retain, or she will be consumed by it."

Most black witches didn't keep familiars. We didn't need them. We gained power through consumption. Of all the lessons I had been taught, the care and keeping of rare familiars hadn't been a footnote in the margin. That was why I treated Colby like a kid, like a *person*, instead of as a pet or a conduit.

After I finished reading the grimoire from cover to cover, I would have more research ahead of me.

"Ha! That means we're a team whether you want to be or not." She was smug as a bug. "You don't get a vote."

"Harsh." I wiggled my lap to make her dance. "Phenomenal cosmic powers are making your head swell."

Launching herself off my knee, she zoomed closer. "Do you know what tonight is?"

"I don't even know what today is."

"It's Halloween." She pirouetted in the air. "Will you take me trick-or-treating?"

"Colby," Clay chided in a gentle tone. "Rue is exhausted. We need to let her rest."

"Hollis Apothecary was supposed to have an open house tonight." I plucked at the covers. "I'm not sure I'm ready to face the store yet. Or the town."

There would be so many questions about the store, the girls, my ex. And I was tired of the lying.

Clutching her hands under her chin, she begged, "Can Clay take me?"

A moth hair accessory didn't look odd on me, but on Clay, folks might stare. "I don't know..."

"Come in costume," Asa suggested to me. "That way, no one will recognize you."

"That's not a terrible idea." I mulled it over. "That would solve a lot of our problems."

Namely that if I wore an actual costume, but kept my present company, everyone would recognize me.

But a glamour could reshape us enough to enjoy a stress-free night out incognito.

"I vote we go as Marie Antoinette," Colby chimed in. "I would look awesome in silver and diamonds."

We shared a costume every year to make blending in easier for her and to keep her close to me.

The Downtown Samford Halloween Spooktacular, which everyone called *the ghost walk* for short, was a lot more fun when you showed up and stuffed your face with free goodies versus having to provide free goodies for others to stuff into their faces.

"Done." I flicked a wrist. "What about you, Clay?"

"Julia Child."

"Always a classic." I skipped to Asa. "Well?"

"The devil."

"Okay." I didn't imagine the twitch in his cheek. "Like red-jump-suit devil?"

"I was thinking more along the lines of this." The transformation gripped him, and his daemon appeared. "Trick-or-treat."

A snort blasted out my nose. "You want to trick-or-treat?"

The daemon ducked his head but nodded once before giving himself back over to Asa.

"How about I glamour the daemon into pajama Satan?" I pursed my lips. "Just to take the edge off."

Plenty of supernaturals let it all hang out in public on Halloween, but the daemon was intense.

Maybe that was the allure. He wanted to blend among normal people and be praised for his appearance rather than feared or shunned for it. Even supernaturals feared Asa and the incredible beast within him.

"That's fine," he agreed without complaint, his eyes brightening.

Apparently, Asa *and* the daemon wanted out for a few hours to celebrate surviving yet another case.

A genuine yawn stretched my jaw, and I shooed them. "Wake me up when it's time to go."

Alone in my room, I did try to sleep, but I must have used my weekly allotment while recovering.

Since I had yet to check my phone, I did that, and I immediately regretted it.

Mayor Tate was already in a snit over "the eyesore".

I assumed she meant my shop.

Her voicemail was one long rant, and I lost interest a few seconds in. The highlights were her blasting me for my poor timing, as if I had planned this to spite her, and her guilting me for ruining the ghost walk for my neighboring stores.

Done with my dose of reality, I tossed my phone, hauled out the grimoire, and began reading.

Despite my choice of bedtime story, I must have dozed off, because a cannonballing moth with plenty of junk in her trunk hit me in the gut in a burst of squeeing excitement that emptied my lungs of oxygen.

Wheezing, certain I was seconds away from dying horribly, I rolled onto my side coughing.

"Get up, get up, get up." She flitted onto my hip. "The ghost walk started ten minutes ago."

"I'm up, I'm up, I'm up." I swung my legs over the side of the bed. "I still smell like pond water."

"If you wanted a shower, you should have gotten up earlier."

"I've created a monster." I nudged her off me. "Fine. You win. I'll go smelling like frog butts."

Good thing we all decided to go in disguise.

"Frog butts." She snickered. "We'll meet you in the kitchen."

Since no one would see the real me, I chose sweats, sneakers, and a baggy tee.

Before I reached the kitchen, I could tell bad news had hit during the few minutes I spent dressing.

With a sob, Colby zipped off to her room and slammed the door behind her.

A long sigh parted Clay's lips as he watched her go, but he didn't follow.

Asa stared at the floor, one hand in his pocket, and took shallow breaths as if trying to calm himself.

"What's wrong?" I thought of the girls and swallowed. "Clay?"

"We've been handed a new case," he explained. "The director wants us on the next flight out of Bama."

"Oh," I said softly, surprised when the ache didn't ease one bit. "I thought you guys would have a day or two to decompress." Black Hats got two days off a week, sick days, and even three weeks paid vacation. Working for the Bureau was, in a lot of ways, like a regular job. "I didn't think to warn Colby."

"We could delay a few hours." Asa's voice came out as a coarse growl. "We could leave in the morning."

"This is why I didn't want you two getting attached, Ace." Clay dragged a hand down his face. "Daemons, in case you haven't noticed, are stage-five clingers." That part was for me before he pivoted back to Asa. "Rue agreed to consult on cases, not reenter the field. I warned you. Both of you. No one ever listens."

Asa lifted his head, his eyes a feral burnt crimson, and his knuckles popped down at his side.

This was not good. Not at all. Not even a little bit.

"We'll work together again," I told Asa. "You've got my number and my address. It's not like I'll vanish."

"You might." He turned that simmering gaze on me. "You have before."

He had me there, but that was before I signed a contract with Black Hat to consult.

"This is my home." I had fought for it and won it. "I'm not leaving."

Proving he was over the drama, Clay swooped in to hug me. "I'll be in touch, Dollface."

"See you later." I clung a beat too long. "Let's not wait ten years to do this again."

Withdrawing, he twitched his lips in a smile. "That depends entirely on you."

The urge to thwack him with my wand surfaced, but it was more likely to break than him.

Turning on his heel, Clay marched from the house to the SUV and climbed in to wait on Asa.

"Well." I scuffed the toe of my sneaker. "This is awkward."

I wasn't sure what I was supposed to say to Asa. I wasn't sure he had anything good to say to me.

"I would like to give you something." He withdrew his hand from his pocket. "Will you accept it?"

"It depends," I hedged, attempting to get a better look at what he held. "What is it?"

"A bracelet." He held it up for me to see. "I made it while you were sleeping."

A narrow black strip dangled from his fingers that reminded me of a braided friendship bracelet. I bet he knitted it, given its detail, but the material was peculiar.

"Okay." I offered him my wrist. "Thank you."

The silky material wrapped three times before he tied it off with an intricate knot.

His warm fingers lingered on my skin. "Can you make me a promise?"

"It depends," I repeated myself. "What is it?"

"Wear this until we see one another again."

That could be years almost popped out of my mouth, but I bit down on the words.

Back on the director's radar, I would be lucky to go another month before he pinged me again.

"I'll wear it for six months." That seemed safe enough. "Deal?"

Challenge gleamed in his eyes. "Deal."

He drew me against him, his grip on my wrist like iron, and embraced me as if this were goodbye forever instead of a few weeks or months. He rested his chin on top of my head, and his chest expanded against mine as he breathed me in. I couldn't help it if my arms snaked around him too. I mean, it was rude not to return hugs, right? I was doing the socially correct thing here.

The scent of him filled my head, and I admired the sleek lines of his muscular back with my fingertips.

"I should go," he breathed, but he didn't budge. "Clay is waiting."

"You should go," I agreed, but I didn't budge either. "Clay has set a timer on his phone by now."

An obnoxious series of honks guaranteed to bring a hungover Mrs. Gleason running made me wince and step back.

"I have a question," I started before I lost my nerve. "What did it mean? You stealing my food?"

For all the concessions I made for him, he could tell me that much.

"Daemon sense potential mates through their saliva." He started toward the door. "We're a match."

"A match?"

"We're biologically compatible," he explained. "It's not a fated-mate connection like wargs share."

"It's just biology." I touched the bracelet. "Okay." I rubbed my wrist. "I understand nature happens."

"And, Rue?" He lingered on the threshold. "When you started playing the game, as a she-daemon would, one who wanted to confirm our compatibility for herself, you granted me permission to pursue you."

The bracelet made my wrist itch all of a sudden, but try as I might, it wouldn't budge for love or money.

Asa crossed the porch and took the stairs at a clip. A less chari-table person might accuse him of running.

"What does this mean?" I held up my wrist and pointed at it. "*Asa.*"

Without glancing back, Asa climbed into the SUV, belted in, and locked the doors.

Locked. The. Doors.

As if that would keep me out if I really wanted in.

Only *after* the SUV turned off my driveway onto the main road did he text me the answer.

>>*The bracelet wards off other males in my absence.*

>*You slapped a chastity belt on me?*

Turning my wrist, searching for the knot he had vanished, I couldn't help but admire the intricate design.

And that was when I noticed what else he had done.

>*This is your hair, isn't it?*

>>*Have fun trick-or-treating, Rue.*

I was still fuming when Colby emerged from her room with droopy antennae and sniffles.

"They're not gone forever." I glared at my wrist. "They'll be back before you know it."

"Promise?"

"I swear it." Asa was going to remove this bracelet, and then I would strangle him with it. "So, Marie?"

"You'll still take me?" Her expression brightened. "Even though Clay and Asa aren't here?"

"Now you've got me craving chocolate." I rubbed my stomach. "You only have yourself to blame."

"I found the perfect dress." She shot toward her rig. "Let me grab the link."

While she skimmed open tabs, I sent Arden and Camber flowers and balloons from the hospital gift shop. It was the least I could do since visiting hours were over for the day. I would have to drop in tomorrow.

An unknown number lit up my phone's screen, and I stepped onto the porch to take the call. "Hello?"

"I understand congratulations are in order."

Gooseflesh raced down my arms. "How good of you to call, Director Nádasdy."

"Please," he said, all jovial good cheer, "call me Grandfather."

"I would rather not call you anything."

A tense silence hung between us, in which I heard the layers peeling back to reveal what lay beneath.

"Elspeth, I have been more than generous in my dealings with you."

"You were *very* generous with your cane when I was younger."

More of his façade crumbled in the quiet. I heard it in the uptick in his breathing.

"I sent it," Colby called out behind me. "Did you see?"

I mashed the mute button, but I was too slow, and the director chuckled into the receiver.

"Colby Timms, I presume." His laughter reminded me of the rustle of old bones. "Tell her I said hello."

Fingers trembling to hear her name on his withered lips, I ended the call and blocked the number.

"Are you okay?" Colby lit on my shoulder. "Who was that?"

"Wrong number." I cleared my throat. "Let me get my kit, and we'll get glamoured up, okay?"

Butting against my jaw, she rubbed her furry head on me in a comforting gesture. "Okay."

I dropped her in the kitchen then headed to my room for supplies. I paused when I noticed the grimoire. I had left it under my pillow. Now it sat in the middle of the bed. I doubted Colby would touch it, and we were alone in the house. As I perched on the edge of the mattress, recalling the director's quiet menace, I was tempted, so tempted, to crack open the book penned in hate to discover answers to my problems.

"I'm not going to use you," I told it, and myself. "The information on Colby is all that interests me."

The grimoire sat there, emanating blackest magic, but it gave no outward indication of sentience.

"I'm glad we got that settled."

The cover left my palms tingling when I lifted it and carried it to my closet to a magically insulated safe.

As I secured the grimoire in with other dark artifacts in my macabre collection of relics too dangerous to entrust into others' care, I reflected on Asa's comment about me punishing myself. Maybe he was right. Maybe I had to hurt, to crave, to *hunger*, in order to keep myself strong enough to resist temptation.

And resist I did.

I might be a Black Hat again, but I was still a white witch.

ABOUT THE AUTHOR

USA Today best-selling author Hailey Edwards writes about questionable applications of otherwise perfectly good magic, the transformative power of love, the family you choose for yourself, and blowing stuff up. Not necessarily all at once. That could get messy.

www.HaileyEdwards.net

ALSO BY HAILEY EDWARDS

How to Rattle an Undead Couple #9

The Potentate of Atlanta

Shadow of Doubt #1

Pack of Lies #2

Change of Heart #3

Proof of Life #4

Moment of Truth #5

Badge of Honor #6

Black Dog Series

Dog with a Bone #1

Dog Days of Summer #1.5

Heir of the Dog #2

Lie Down with Dogs #3

Old Dog, New Tricks #4

Black Dog Series Novellas

Stone-Cold Fox

Gemini Series

Dead in the Water #1

Head Above Water #2

Hell or High Water #3

Gemini Series Novellas

Fish Out of Water

Lorimar Pack Series

Promise the Moon #1

Wolf at the Door #2

Over the Moon #3

Araneae Nation

A Heart of Ice #.5

A Hint of Frost #1

A Feast of Souls #2

A Cast of Shadows #2.5

A Time of Dying #3

A Kiss of Venom #3.5

A Breath of Winter #4

A Veil of Secrets #5

Daughters of Askara

Everlong #1

Evermine #2

Eversworn #3

Wicked Kin

Soul Weaver #1

Printed in Great Britain
by Amazon

33109955R00128